the Clerk

for Linnet's Book.

The clerk led him over to the Romances. She handed Linnet's book to Jon, who took it gingerly.

From the look on his face, Linnet told herself, you'd have thought he'd just been handed a poisonous snake.

The clerk gave Jon a curious look as she rang up the sale. "We don't have many men customers buying Romances. Do you mind if I ask you why you're buying it?"

"For penance." Jon walked back over to Linnet. "Satisfied?" he asked. "I feel like an utter fool."

"Good," Linnet told him laughingly.

"At least she put it in a bag," Jon said. "Imagine how I'd feel if someone I knew saw me carrying this."

THEA LOVAN

was a history major in college and always had a consuming interest in faraway people and places. She works now as a travel writer and has visited some of the most exotic corners of the world.

Dear Reader:

I'd like to take this opportunity to thank you for all your support and encouragement of Silhouette Romances.

Many of you write in regularly, telling us what you like best about Silhouette, which authors are your favorites. This is a tremendous help to us as we strive to publish the best contemporary romances possible.

All the romances from Silhouette Books are for you, so enjoy this book and the many stories to come.

Karen Solem
Editor-in-Chief
Silhouette Books

THEA LOVAN
A Story
Well Told

Silhouette Romance

Published by Silhouette Books New York

America's Publisher of Contemporary Romance

Silhouette Books by Thea Lovan

Passionate Journey (DES #28)
A Tender Passion (ROM #281)
A Story Well Told (ROM #326)

SILHOUETTE BOOKS, a Division of Simon & Schuster, Inc.
1230 Avenue of the Americas, New York, N.Y. 10020

Distributed by Pocket Books.

ISBN: 0-671-57326-8

First Silhouette Books printing October, 1984

10 9 8 7 6 5 4 3 2 1

Map by Ray Lundgren

America's Publisher of Contemporary Romance

Printed in the U.S.A.

BC91

To my mother, the first Thea

A Story
Well Told

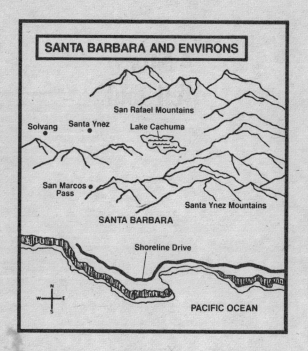

SANTA BARBARA AND ENVIRONS

San Rafael Mountains

Solvang   Santa Ynez   Lake Cachuma

San Marcos Pass

Santa Ynez Mountains

SANTA BARBARA

Shoreline Drive

PACIFIC OCEAN

Chapter One

"I've never wanted another woman as much as I want you," Brad muttered. "Come here."

Joanna crossed the room. She raised her eyes pleadingly to his. Don't do this, they seemed to beg him, expressing the words she was powerless to say.

Brad ignored her unspoken plea. He crushed her lips beneath his own and, as his tongue forced its way into her mouth, Joanna began to struggle in a weak, ineffectual way.

"Don't fight me," Brad growled. "You're mine and I'm going to prove it."

"I can't," she whispered incoherently as his hands began traveling over her body.

He swept her into his arms and carried her toward the bedroom. "You can," he said, "and you will."

* * *

"No! No! NO!" Linnet said aloud as she ripped the paper from her typewriter. What was wrong with Brad? Where was his sensitivity? His understanding? He was treating Joanna with an arrogance, a high-handedness no woman deserved. As for Joanna, she was behaving like a complete idiot. Where was her pride? Her dignity?

In disgust Linnet crumpled the paper into a ball and hurled it into the overflowing wastebasket. She pushed back her chair and wandered aimlessly around the living room of her Santa Barbara house.

It wasn't Brad's fault that he had suddenly grown into such a miserable example of manhood. And it wasn't Joanna's fault that she was such a spineless ninny. It was Linnet's fault—and no one else's. For some reason, she was suddenly unable to make her characters behave the way they should.

Linnet Brooks was a well-known romance writer who had been turning out four books a year for the past four years. And not once in all those sixteen books had her characters behaved so abominably. It was almost as if Brad and Joanna had minds of their own and were going to behave as they pleased regardless of Linnet's attempts to make them more likable.

She flung herself down in a chair and drummed her fingers impatiently on the arm. What was she going to do with them? Her readers would never like Brad and Joanna if they continued to behave like this. She didn't like them herself.

Absently Linnet glanced at the clock, looked again, then jumped to her feet. She had been so engrossed in the problem of Brad and Joanna that she had let the time get away from her. Glenn was waiting for her in the small waterfront area near Santa Barbara's Cabrillo Boulevard.

She hastily ran a comb through her long, dark hair,

hurried out of her small, Spanish-style house, and hopped into her car. She knew she had to hurry. If she didn't, he would think she wasn't coming and go home.

She parked her car and walked quickly along the sidewalk until she saw him sitting on a bench in the shade of a palm tree. In front of him the Pacific stretched endlessly; behind him Santa Barbara sat basking in the summer sunlight.

"I'm sorry I'm late," she said, giving him a light kiss on the cheek. "Somehow the time got away from me."

"I don't mind." His eyes twinkled at her from under their shaggy white brows. "It isn't every old man who gets to wait for a beautiful young woman."

"You aren't old," Linnet told him. "Not in the ways that count."

"I'm old enough to be your grandfather," he reminded her.

"And I wish you were," she said as she sat down beside him.

He was touched. She reminded him so much of his wife Amy. Aimée, he had called her, giving her name a French twist and a special meaning. Amy . . . his love and the center of his life until she had died five years before. One day he'd tell Linnet about Amy, but not today. Today he could see that Linnet needed to talk of the present.

"Are Brad and Joanna giving you more trouble?" he asked shrewdly. They had discussed her work before. He knew of the difficulties she had been having with this book.

Linnet sighed. "They certainly are. *A Summer Rhapsody* has been nothing but trouble since the day I started it." She stared out over the blue Pacific. "Sometimes I think I should throw it away and start over."

"Why don't you?" he suggested. "Or at least put it aside

for a few weeks. People in other professions suffer from burnout. Why not writers?"

He watched her with enjoyment. The quality of his days had improved enormously since he had made the acquaintance of this beautiful young woman. Beautiful and, he judged, fragile. Oh, she seemed poised and self-confident enough. But there was a vulnerability to her, a vulnerability that she kept well hidden. It intrigued him. Physically, the combination of her dark hair, alabaster skin, and soft blue eyes made her a pleasure to look at.

Her features were good, but they weren't what gave Linnet her beauty, Glenn thought. Her beauty came from her nature. Not many young women as attractive and talented as Linnet would care to spend a part of each day with a tired old man, he thought.

"He just isn't behaving the way he should," Linnet burst out in exasperation. She looked at the frail old man sitting beside her. "Brad, I mean."

He nodded. He knew who she meant. Aside from the heroes in her books, there seemed to be no men in her life. In fact, he didn't think she'd as much as mentioned the name of a man in all the weeks they had been meeting. It was a waste, he thought, but Linnet apparently wanted it no other way.

"I've pushed him, pulled him, I've done everything I can think of," Linnet went on, oblivious to Glenn's thoughts. "I still can't get him to behave the way I want him to."

Glenn's eyes twinkled. "Put the book aside for a few weeks," he urged her. "He's sure to come around sooner or later."

Linnet shook her head. "I don't know if that's such a good idea. I might lose him entirely, or at least the essence of him. Besides, I have a deadline to meet." She fell silent, staring broodingly over the Pacific. "It's not Brad's fault," she said softly. "It's my fault. I don't know what's wrong with me. I've never had so much trouble with a man."

"Perhaps that *is* the trouble," Glenn said, picking his words carefully. "He isn't a real man. He's just a figment of your imagination. You've allowed him to become real and now he's doing what he wants instead of letting you control him."

Linnet smiled sheepishly. "You may be right. I do take my characters seriously."

"Too seriously," Glenn said firmly. "You need a real man. I wish you'd let me introduce you to Jon, my grandson. He . . ."

"That's very sweet of you," Linnet interrupted hastily, "but I just don't have time for a man in my life right now." And if I did, she thought to herself, it wouldn't be Jon West.

It was obvious that Glenn doted on his grandson. Everything he had said about him was complimentary—too complimentary, Linnet thought cynically. Glenn praised his grandson in glowing terms. Jon knew the best restaurants, Jon's opinion on the Middle East was worth twice what the politicians had to say, Jon was an expert tennis player and golfer. As far as Linnet was concerned, Jon sounded too good to be true. She had no desire to meet him.

Tactfully, though, she didn't let Glenn know what she thought of his grandson. She knew the old man and his wife had raised Jon after the death of Jon's parents. His devotion was understandable.

But what did it get him? Linnet asked herself. From what she could gather, Jon had very little time for his grandfather. He didn't see the old man very often and, even worse, he let the old man live in near poverty. Glenn's clothing was worn, almost shabby, and Linnet knew he had to live nearby, somewhere within walking distance of the water-front. The apartment buildings there were old and run-down, and Linnet hated to think of Glenn living in one of them.

He's such a darling old man, Linnet thought. If he were my grandfather, I'd see that he lacked for nothing. She supposed Jon spent all his money on wine, women, and song. He sounded to her like the type who would do just that. She wouldn't even put it past him to try and borrow money from his impecunious grandfather.

No, Jon West definitely was not the stuff her heroes were made of. He wouldn't be allowed into her romance novels, and she certainly wasn't going to let him into her life.

"When are you going to have time for a man in your life?" Glenn was asking.

Linnet laughed. She was used to Glenn trying to play matchmaker. For some reason, he seemed to think that she and his grandson would make a perfect couple.

"I have to finish this book soon," she told him teasingly. "And then . . ."

"And then you'll have another book to do, and another," he finished for her. "I know you love your work. But you're young and beautiful. Aren't you interested in having a social life at all?"

"I go out now and then," Linnet told him, "but I don't want to be seriously involved with anyone right now."

He looked at her thoughtfully. "You never want to be seriously involved with anyone," he pointed out finally. "Did you have a bad experience with a man?"

She shook her head. "No," she said lightly. "Nothing like that. I've just been too busy writing."

It was her sister who had had the bad experience, Linnet thought, not her. Unhappy at home with her father and stepmother after Linnet had gone to college, Gail had married young. As soon as she had gotten pregnant, her husband had run out on her, leaving her with no money and a child on the way. Linnet, then working as a secretary during the day and writing at night, had willingly taken her in.

Now, a few years later, Gail had a second husband, a man who provided far more financial than emotional support. Though Gail seemed content enough, Linnet's heart ached every time she thought of her sister. In two marriages, Gail still hadn't found the love Linnet believed in so fervently, the love she wrote about in her books.

Linnet was not foolish enough to let her sister's experience sour her on love. But it had taught her that real life almost never had the happy endings of her books. She was holding out for a happy ending.

"I still wish you'd let me introduce you to Jon," Glenn said regretfully.

Linnet laughed again. "Don't you know fix-ups never work? Besides, he probably wouldn't be interested in someone like me."

"Oh, he'd be interested, all right. You're beautiful enough to interest any man. But I won't force it. If you don't want to meet him, you don't have to."

"I'd rather spend my time with you," Linnet said.

She was telling the truth. Glenn West gave her something she had missed by not being around her grandparents, and she cherished it.

As a child, there had been a definite lack of permanence, of stability, in Linnet's life. Her mother had died soon after Gail's birth. Her father, an executive with a large corporation, had been required to move almost yearly. Though he eventually remarried, Linnet's stepmother did not provide the security the two girls needed. New children, her children, soon came along to occupy her time and attention.

It was probably not fair, Linnet thought now that she was older, but as a child she had felt like an outsider and she knew her sister had too. At eighteen, convinced she was valuable to her father and stepmother only as a baby-sitter, she had gone away to college.

After college she had moved to Santa Barbara, a town she had fallen in love with years earlier when her family had lived briefly in Los Angeles. She worked as a secretary until she had sold two books, then she had devoted herself to writing full time.

With success had come money, and she had bought a house. She was determined to put down roots, to make a home for herself. Glenn was helping her.

"I'm flattered that you like to spend time with me," he answered, "but I think you'd be better off with people your own age."

"I see plenty of people my own age," she reassured him. "I go to parties and occasionally I even go out on dates."

He smiled at the teasing tone of her voice. "I'm glad to hear that. And now, I think you'd better be going. It's getting late."

Linnet glanced down at the watch on her wrist, the watch that seemed to control her life. She lived by the clock and by deadlines. For a moment she felt the urge to rebel, to ignore the time and let hours, even days and weeks, slip by. Then her discipline took over.

"You're right," she said regretfully. The time she spent talking to Glenn always went too quickly. "I have to get back to Brad and Joanna. Are you leaving now?"

"Not quite yet," he told her. "I've got my bread crumbs. I think I'll stay here a few more minutes and feed the birds."

It was a ritual. He was always there before Linnet arrived and he always left after she did. It was almost as though he planned it that way. She had occasionally wondered why he never left with her. He probably had nothing else to do, she reasoned, and he did seem to enjoy feeding the birds.

"Don't stay too much longer," she said. "It's going to be hot today." She stopped herself from saying more. Glenn didn't like it when she fussed over him.

She hurried back to her car, wishing she had more time to spend with him. She turned back once to look at him. He looked so lonely sitting by himself on the bench overlooking the ocean.

If only that grandson of his . . . She shook her head and turned resolutely back toward her car. Glenn would be annoyed if he knew she was worrying about him. Besides, she had to get back to Brad and Joanna. Somehow she had to get them back on the track.

The next day, Linnet was up early. She still wasn't completely satisfied with Brad and Joanna, but at least she had made progress: they had decided to behave with a show of decency. Much to her relief, Brad was no longer trying to bully Joanna into the bedroom, and Joanna was acting like a woman instead of an embarrassed teenager. Even better, though, was the decision she had made late last night. Glenn was right. She needed a break and, after four years of hard work, she was going to take one. Why not, she thought happily as she crossed the street to the small grassy area overlooking the ocean. She deserved it.

It was a bright summer day and already the Santa Barbara sun was hot. Linnet was glad of the cool relief of the palm trees. She scanned the benches near the water, looking anxiously for Glenn. Though she looked forward to seeing him each day, she wasn't sure it was good for him to be out on a hot day like this. He was so old and frail looking.

When she didn't spot him, she sank down on one of the benches overlooking the Pacific and let the breeze off the water cool her. Perhaps it would be better if he didn't come, she thought. Sitting in this heat might be too much for him, not to mention the walk getting there. Not for the first time,

Linnet wished she knew where he lived. Except for that grandson of his, he was all alone, and she worried about him. He wouldn't tell her where he lived, though. In fact, he wouldn't say much about himself at all.

Sitting there, Linnet thought about the first time they had met. It had been nearly three months ago. She had come down to the waterfront hoping for an inspiration. Even then Brad and Joanna had been giving her trouble. There were times when Linnet thought they would be with her forever. She worked and worked on *A Summer Rhapsody,* but it never seemed any closer to completion.

She hadn't found inspiration, but she had found something better. Sitting on the same bench she was sitting on today, there had been an old man feeding the seagulls. Linnet had sat down beside him, and before long they had struck up a conversation.

Now, their meetings had become a habit. They talked about everything, particularly her work. Though Glenn had no writing experience, he had some penetrating insights into the human heart. His comments and observations were almost always to the point. Besides, just talking about her book helped clarify things in Linnet's mind.

She looked around again, wondering if she could have missed him. It wasn't like him to be late. Sure enough, she saw him walking toward her, leaning a little more heavily than usual on his walking stick. Linnet jumped up and ran to meet him.

"I'm sorry I'm late," he said. "This heat slowed me down."

"I was afraid you weren't coming," she told him as she kissed him on the cheek.

"I wouldn't miss my visit with you." His smile seemed a little forced.

Linnet took his arm.

The heat was bothering him, she thought worriedly. He

looked a little shaky. He should not have come out on a day like this.

"Let's sit over here," she suggested, leading him to a bench standing in the shade of a tall palm tree. "It won't be quite so hot."

He sat down gratefully, took off his hat, and fanned himself with it.

"Perhaps you shouldn't have come," Linnet said anxiously. Now that he was out of the sun, she was worried about the flushed look of his face. All at once, he seemed even more frail than usual.

"Perhaps not," he admitted. "The sun is hotter than I thought. But I don't get to see many young people any more. I look forward to our talks," he added with a simplicity that caught at her heart.

"So do I," she said, patting his hand.

That grandson of his, she thought wrathfully. She could never think of him as Jon. He was always "that grandson" in a way that wasn't complimentary. If he'd pay more attention to the old man, Glenn wouldn't be so starved for company.

"But you know I'd be happy to come to your apartment. There's no need for you to come here every day."

"Oh no!" He sounded genuinely shocked. "That would never do."

The sound of his voice made Linnet wonder anew about his apartment. She hated to think of him living in a place so run-down and dingy that he was embarrassed to have visitors.

"As long as I can meet you here, I will. After that . . ." He took a deep breath. "We'll let the future take care of itself."

Linnet blinked back the tears that suddenly filled her eyes.

"Speaking of the future," she said in a determinedly

cheerful voice, "there is something I want to talk to you about."

He looked at her expectantly.

"I thought about what you said yesterday and I think you're right. I do need to get away for a while."

His eyes twinkled at her. "I thought you were going to tell me you had decided to let me introduce you to Jon."

Never that, Linnet thought, though she didn't say it.

"One thing at a time," she said instead. "Right now I don't need a man in my life. I need some rest and relaxation. Do you realize I haven't had a vacation since I was in college? And since I worked during the summers, I wouldn't even call that a vacation," she added.

"Then you deserve one. When are you going?"

"This weekend, I hope. As soon as I can make the arrangements."

She thought the light in his eyes dimmed a little and she was touched to think he'd miss her.

"I'll miss you, of course," he said, confirming her thoughts. "But I know you need to get away."

"That's what I want to talk to you about," she said eagerly. "I want you to come with me." She had wanted to do something for him for weeks but she had been afraid of hurting his pride. This, she thought, was the perfect opportunity for getting him out of the heat of the city. If that grandson wouldn't do something for Glenn, then she would.

"Me?" He was genuinely astonished.

"You," she repeated firmly. "Why not? I'm going to rent a house in Carmel, and you could keep me company."

Surprise and pleasure showed on his face. "Are you sure you want me to come?" he asked. "Wouldn't I be in the way?"

He sounded rather wistful, Linnet thought. It was all the fault of that grandson of his. He probably never wanted his grandfather around. He probably thought the old man would cramp his style, she thought scornfully.

"Of course you wouldn't be in the way," she told him warmly. "I'd love having you. You know," she confessed a little shyly, "I think of you as the grandfather I never had."

He covered her hand with his gnarled one. "You couldn't say anything nicer to an old man," he told her.

The look on his face made Linnet want to cry. She didn't suppose he felt needed or wanted much any more.

"Please say you'll come," she urged him. "It would mean so much to me." She couldn't bear to think of him suffering through the heat of the summer in the city. She wasn't even sure his apartment was air-conditioned.

"If you're sure you want me," he said hesitantly, "I'll come."

"Wonderful," Linnet exclaimed. She thought Glenn suddenly looked ten years younger.

"On one condition," he was saying.

It was her turn to look expectant.

"My birthday is on the twenty-eighth."

"That's two days from now," Linnet put in.

"That's right, Thursday. I'd like you to have dinner with me to celebrate. It will be my treat to both of us."

"I'd love to," Linnet said. "But you must let me take you to dinner. It's hardly fair for you to have to pick up the tab on your birthday." She wasn't at all sure he could afford to take her to dinner. She didn't want him to have to do without anything in order to take her out somewhere.

"That's nice of you, but it's my birthday and my dinner," he said firmly.

Linnet started to say something else, but he held up his hand.

"It's all settled," he said with a flash of imperiousness. "We won't discuss it any more."

Linnet smiled to herself and wondered, not for the first time, what kind of past he had had. She knew better than to ask. For some reason, he didn't want to talk about himself. Linnet had previously asked what she thought were tactfully worded questions, only to have them courteously turned away. As a result, much of his life remained a mystery.

Now she acquiesced to his wishes gracefully. She had no desire to hurt his pride.

"In that case, thank you very much. I'll look forward to it. Thursday evening?"

"Yes. I'll make reservations at the Chez Nous. Jon says it's the best in town."

And the most expensive, Linnet thought unhappily. How was Glenn going to be able to afford such a place?

"Wouldn't you like some place a little more informal?" she asked.

"We can relax in Carmel." The twinkle was back in his eyes. "For my birthday I want the best. Is it a date?"

"It's a date," she told him, wondering if she could get away with ordering only a salad. She could tell him she was on a diet.

"Good. It will be a pleasure for me to step out with a beautiful woman on my arm," he told her gallantly.

Linnet blushed slightly. She knew she was attractive; she'd been told so many times before. But somehow it meant more to her coming from this old man.

"Would you like to meet there or shall I pick you up?" he asked.

"Let's meet there." That would save him part of the taxi fare. She was sure he didn't have a car, and she doubted if he was strong enough to drive one if he did.

"Or I could pick you up," she said, knowing her offer would be refused. It was. He seemed determined to keep her from seeing his apartment.

"We'll meet there," he said firmly. "Is six-thirty all

right? I know it's not fashionable to eat so early, but I'm too old to eat much later.''

''Six-thirty is fine. What about your grandson?'' she asked suddenly. ''Won't he want to have dinner with you on such a special occasion?''

''Jon? I'm sure he would,'' Glenn said quickly, ''but he'll be out of town.''

Linnet bit the inside of her lip. Jon should postpone his trip, she told herself, and spend the day with his grandfather. The old man wouldn't be having too many more birthdays. She didn't want to say what she was thinking for fear of upsetting Glenn. He was devoted to his grandson, though, in Linnet's opinion, Jon didn't deserve even a fraction of his grandfather's devotion.

''Look at the time,'' Glenn exclaimed regretfully. ''You had better get back to work.''

Linnet got to her feet reluctantly. She didn't like the idea of leaving him. He still looked flushed to her and she couldn't help being concerned.

''Are you sure you'll be all right?'' she asked anxiously.

He waved away her concern. ''I'll be fine.''

''Then I'll see you tomorrow,'' Linnet said. If only he would let her see him home, she thought unhappily.

''I'll be here as usual,'' Glenn told her.

But he wasn't there as usual. Linnet waited for him for nearly an hour. Finally, convinced that he wasn't coming, she went home and worried.

He wasn't there the next day either.

He's resting up for our dinner date this evening, Linnet told herself as she wrapped the two books she had bought him as a birthday gift. She didn't believe her own words. She had the feeling something was wrong. Even more than ever, she wished she had gotten him to give her his phone number, at least.

She dressed carefully for her dinner date, not knowing

what else to do. The restaurant was her only link with him. She wanted him to be proud of her as they walked into the restaurant together—if they walked into the restaurant together, she thought unhappily.

Instead of leaving her long, dark hair loose as she usually did, she wound it in a careful coil on top of her head. The dress she had chosen to wear was a sophisticated one. It was white, to bring out what little tan she had managed to acquire, with simple, classic lines. She brushed on a little extra eye makeup and blush, knowing from experience that the Chez Nous would be dark. Finally, she put on small diamond stud earrings—a present to herself after she had sold her third book. She left her neck bare.

The dress didn't really need jewelry, she thought as she gave herself a last glance in the mirror. Its understated elegance suited her perfectly.

She arrived at the restaurant promptly at six-thirty and looked around anxiously for Glenn. He wasn't there. Though she hadn't really expected to see him, her heart sank.

"I'm meeting Mr. West for dinner," she told the maitre d'.

"Monsieur West? He hasn't arrived yet," the maitre d' said, giving her an approving smile. "Shall I show you to your table or would you like to wait here?"

"I'll wait here," she said, clutching the gaily wrapped package she had brought with her.

She stood as far out of the way as she could while she waited for Glenn. As the minutes ticked by, her worry changed to fear. It wasn't like Glenn to be late. He was scrupulously punctual. A few more minutes went by and she was even more alarmed. Something had happened to him, something serious. Nothing else would have made him so late. She approached the maitre d'.

"Did you get a telephone number from Mr. West when he made the reservation?" she asked.

How she wished she had insisted that he give her his phone number. She had no idea how to reach him, how to help him. What if he was alone in his apartment, sick and unable to call for help? At that thought her heart almost stopped beating.

The man checked his reservation book. "No," he said, "no telephone number. Mademoiselle should not worry. I'm sure he will be here soon. Let me show you to your table. Perhaps a drink . . . ?"

Linnet shook her head. What should she do now?

The maitre d' looked past her. "You see?" he exclaimed. "I said mademoiselle had no need to worry. Here he is now."

As Linnet turned around to greet Glenn, a great feeling of relief swept over her. But she couldn't see him. Blocking her view of the door was a tall man, slender hipped, with strong, broad shoulders. If Linnet hadn't been so anxious to see for herself that Glenn was all right, she would have given the man in front of her a second glance, for he had the look of one of her heroes. He had the same quiet confidence and the same startling good looks as the men she wrote about. The only difference was in his hair. Her heroes almost always had dark hair, while this man had thick, straight hair that was not gray but a vibrant silver. It gave his rugged features a certain distinction that dark hair might have obscured. Without the unusual silver hair he would have been extremely attractive; with it, he was devastating. His very presence caused several of the women in the restaurant to look toward the door.

Annoyed, Linnet tried to look past him. He had no right to be so big, so vital, she thought unreasonably. Above all, he had no right to fill the room with his presence. She hoped

Glenn wasn't standing behind him feeling insignificant. For Glenn was nothing like this tall, good-looking man striding toward her.

She tried to move out of his way, to get around him so that she could find Glenn. She felt she had to see for herself that he was all right.

The voice of the maitre d' stopped her.

"Monsieur West," he murmured a little unctuously, "the lady was growing worried."

Monsieur West? Linnet thought. There was apparently some kind of mix-up. The maitre d' had turned to her expectantly while the other man, the other Mr. West, looked at her with obvious surprise.

"Are you Linnet Brooks?" he asked as though he found it hard to believe.

She can't be, he was thinking as he continued to stare at her incredulously. Not only was she beautiful, but there was something . . . special about her.

Jon had been expecting anything but this elegant, rather unapproachable-looking young woman. When his grandfather had confided that he was meeting a woman each day, he had never imagined anyone like this.

So this is Linnet Brooks, he thought. She was the kind of woman who appealed to him: sophisticated, poised, with something extra thrown in. He didn't know what that something extra was, but it made him want to take her in his arms and kiss away the worry and fear in her eyes.

He frowned as he realized what he was thinking and the frown gave his face a harsh severity.

Linnet moved backward involuntarily as she caught sight of the frown. The truth was beginning to dawn on her.

"Are you Jon?" she asked faintly.

She had never imagined he would be so big or so good-looking, and she had certainly never imagined she would react to him like one of the heroines in her books.

With one glance into his eyes, her heart had begun to beat quickly and her knees felt weak.

They stared at each other in silence, communicating in a wordless manner that alarmed Linnet. If it hadn't been for Glenn, she would have turned and walked away. This man could be dangerous!

Chapter Two

"Where is Glenn?" Linnet demanded. "Has anything happened to him?"

"He's ill," Jon said briefly. He was still staring at her in a way Linnet didn't understand.

Even though this was what she had expected, something clutched at Linnet's heart.

"Ill?" she echoed softly. She felt the world sway for a minute, and she realized just how much the old man had come to mean to her.

Jon took her arm to steady her, and the maitre d' began to make clucking noises.

"Perhaps mademoiselle should sit down," he said, hovering over her.

His concern was not only for her, Linnet realized. The other diners were looking at them curiously.

"I'm all right," she told him. She removed her arm from

Jon's grasp. There was something curiously personal about his touch. Even at a time like this, it disturbed her.

"What about Glenn? What happened? Where is he? I want to see him."

"Let's go outside," Jon said.

The maitre d' heaved what sounded like a sigh of relief.

"We can talk on the way to the hospital."

"The hospital? It's serious then."

"Serious enough. It's his heart," Jon told her as he held the heavy door open.

They paused for a moment in front of the restaurant. Linnet clutched Glenn's birthday gift to her chest and shivered slightly, even though the evening was a warm one.

"He'd like to see you," Jon added. "If you feel up to it, that is."

"Of course I feel up to it," Linnet told him impatiently. "I have my car. If you'll tell me which hospital, I'll meet you there."

"You're in no condition to drive. I'll take you," he said brusquely. "You can pick up your car in the morning."

Linnet started to protest but thought better of it. She didn't want to waste precious time standing on the sidewalk arguing when she could be on her way to see Glenn.

Besides, Jon was right. Her hands were shaking so much she wasn't sure she could maneuver the car.

His heart, she thought with horror. That was serious, deadly serious.

"Did he have a heart attack?" she asked as Jon ushered her into his car. It was a sports car, Linnet noted absently, low and sleek.

"Yes," Jon answered as he concentrated on getting the car out of the parking space he had managed to create between two large cars.

"When?"

"Tuesday evening."

Tuesday evening, Linnet thought. She stared out the window, not even seeing the streets that flashed by. That was why he hadn't been down by the ocean yesterday or today. If only she had known, she could have been with him.

"He called me Tuesday evening," Jon went on, "complaining about chest pains. I immediately called the doctor, and he arranged for an ambulance to take Grandfather to the hospital."

Linnet's face, pale and worried looking, was affecting him strangely. He wanted to hold her, to comfort her. The feeling angered him, making his voice harsher than it would have been otherwise.

"I thought you were out of town," Linnet said in surprise.

"I was, but I always leave my grandfather a number where he can reach me," Jon said.

Decent of you, Linnet thought sarcastically. Jon might not spend much time with his grandfather but he always made sure he could be reached by telephone.

"How is he now?" she asked. Glenn was her main concern, not this good-looking man whose strong hands were skillfully piloting the car in and out of the traffic. Linnet looked away from his hands and concentrated on his words. She didn't want to think of his hands, didn't want to think of him at all.

"He's better," Jon said. The relief in his voice was obvious. "Apparently it was only a minor heart attack. A warning, the doctor said."

A warning, Linnet thought. It came as no real surprise to her. Glenn had looked rather shaky when she had left him Tuesday morning. She was still reproaching herself, blaming herself bitterly for not having talked him into giving her his telephone number. She could have been with him the last two days if she had known. Instead, he'd only had this grandson of his, the grandson who didn't care enough about his grandfather to spend his birthday with him.

". . . and he does seem better," Jon was saying.

Linnet switched her attention back to Jon. It could be important.

"When he realized this was Thursday night, he insisted that I get in touch with you to tell you what had happened. I tried to call you, but apparently you had already left."

"I left early," Linnet told him. Her voice shook a little. "I wanted to be sure I was on time. I didn't want him to have to wait for me."

In the semidarkness of the car, Jon gave her a speculative look. Linnet noticed it out of the corner of her eye but paid no attention. She didn't really care what he thought. Not now. Now all she could think about was the old man lying in a hospital room.

"Aren't we there yet?" she asked. It seemed as though they had been driving for hours.

"It will be just a few more minutes," he told her.

"I will be able to see him, won't I?"

In the semidarkness she could see a grim smile on his face and wondered what it meant.

"Under normal circumstances, patients in intensive care can only be seen by relatives. But you won't have any problem getting in. Grandfather has already told the doctor that he intends to see you. The doctor started to refuse, but Grandfather got his way, as usual."

He intercepted the surprised look Linnet gave him. Somehow she couldn't imagine Glenn West throwing his weight around. Then she remembered the occasional flashes of imperiousness she had seen, and her expression changed to one of doubt. Perhaps he wasn't quite what he seemed. Certainly this grandson of his wasn't what Linnet had expected.

A silence fell. There didn't seem to be anything more to say. It wasn't a comfortable silence. As they drove toward the lights of the hospital, Linnet studied Jon's face carefully. For some reason, he looked familiar. She was sure they had never met; her novelist's eye wouldn't have let her forget that face. But still, she had the feeling she had seen him before, or at least a picture of him.

Jon had barely stopped the car before Linnet was running across the parking lot. She checked with the nurse at the reception desk for Glenn's room number and was waiting impatiently for the elevator when Jon caught up with her. He gave her a strange look but said nothing until he had ushered her into his grandfather's room.

"Here she is, Grandfather," he announced cheerfully. "I told you I'd find her and I did."

"I'm sorry I couldn't make it to our dinner," Glenn said to Linnet in a weak voice, "but as you can see . . ." He gestured around him.

Linnet forced herself to smile at him, forced herself not to notice the machines that monitored his heart and his respiration. The sight of him attached to those machines drove home how much he had come to mean to her.

"Well, it is your birthday," she said lightly. "Who am I to argue about where you choose to spend it?"

He was propped up by several pillows, she noticed, and his color was better than she had expected. She relaxed a little.

"It isn't exactly the Chez Nous, is it?" he asked with a note of chagrin in his voice.

"No," she told him, "but it's probably cheaper."

That brought a smile to the old man's face and with it, Linnet relaxed even more. Though he was sick enough, he obviously wasn't as sick as she had feared.

"I brought you a birthday present," Linnet told him.

Behind her she could feel, rather than see, Jon settling into a chair in a corner of the room. He seemed to be watching them a little disapprovingly, though Linnet couldn't imagine why.

Apparently he had no intention of joining in their conversation, and for that Linnet was grateful. She didn't think she liked him very much. There was something about him . . .

"What is it?" Glenn asked. He was obviously touched by her gesture.

"Open it and see."

Carefully Linnet laid the package in his lap. When she saw how Glenn's fingers fumbled with the ribbon and wrapping paper, she helped him with it. He wasn't as strong as that twinkle in his eyes indicated.

Finally the paper had been removed, leaving two large books. Glenn looked at each of them without a word. There was a smile on his face. It was a weak smile, but a smile nonetheless.

"I know you like to read," Linnet said uncertainly. Though she was glad to see him smiling, she was confused by the look on his face. Had she made some kind of mistake? "So I picked up these two biographies by Jonathan Weston. I thought you'd enjoy them, since you're interested in American history.

Jonathan Weston was a well-known biographer of historical figures. His books were considered to be highbrow and brought him more critical acclaim than money. Linnet had read all of the Weston books and had enjoyed them, but she knew many people who found them dry and a bit heavy going. She knew even more people who simply left them lying around, hoping their friends and neighbors would see them and be impressed.

"This is Weston's newest book." The silence in the

room seemed to have changed, though she didn't know why. She had the odd feeling that Glenn was trying hard not to laugh. "It's a biography of John Adams. The other one, about Alexander Hamilton, was written several years ago."

"Have you read them?" Jon asked suddenly from his corner of the room.

His question surprised her. She wouldn't have thought he would be interested in this kind of book, though now that she thought about it, she wasn't at all sure what would interest him.

"I've read the one on Alexander Hamilton," she answered. "I've been saving the other one for my vacation in Carmel."

Jon walked across the room to the other side of the bed on which his grandfather was lying. He picked up one of the books and lifted it as though he were judging its worth by its weight.

"You surprise me," he said. "I thought Grandfather told me you were a romance writer."

There was just the faintest hint of a sneer in his voice. Linnet recognized it at once. She had heard it many times before in the voices of people, particularly men, who considered themselves above reading a love story.

"I *am* a romance writer," Linnet returned evenly. "Does that mean I can't read other books?"

He shrugged. "I just wouldn't think you'd want to. The kind of thing you write hardly has anything in common with political biographies."

Linnet bit off the reply that sprang to her lips. This was no place to get into an argument over the merits of different kinds of literature.

"Have you read them?" she asked instead, making her voice sweet. "From what I've heard of you, books of this kind certainly don't seem like your cup of tea."

Her eyes gazed at him so innocently that he almost missed the subtle insult . . . almost, but not quite. His eyes narrowed in annoyance and the two of them stared at each other over the bed. For a moment they seemed to forget about Glenn; then he turned one of the books over and Linnet looked down.

On the back was a picture of the author. She stared at it for a moment, then looked across the bed to the man who was watching her a little angrily. They were the same man. Jon West . . . Jonathan Weston. She should have known.

Linnet felt her face turn pink and wished she could drop through the floor. No wonder Jon's face had seemed familiar. She glanced back down at the picture on the dust cover. It didn't do him justice. Perhaps that was why she hadn't put the two together at once. The picture didn't come close to capturing the vitality Jon conveyed in person.

"Do you mean to tell me," Jon was asking incredulously, "that when you bought these you honestly didn't know that I wrote them?"

"Of course not." She felt more than a little foolish. Perhaps she should have realized it. "How would I have known?"

"By the name, for one thing." His voice was dry.

"The two names are similar, I grant you that. But they aren't the same. It never occurred to me that you and the writer Jonathan Weston were the same person."

Jon turned to his grandfather. "You didn't tell her?"

"I didn't see any reason to," he said mildly. "It never seemed to come up."

That puzzled Linnet. Why hadn't Glenn told her that his grandson was the well-known and respected writer Jonathan Weston? He had told her everything else he could think of to get her to meet him. Yet he had left out the one thing that might have piqued her interest. She wondered why.

Abruptly Jon left his side of the bed and crossed the room. Linnet turned and saw him speak in low tones to a doctor. She took the opportunity to talk privately to Glenn.

"I think I should leave now," she said. "I don't want to tire you." It seemed to her that his face had lost what little color it had had when she walked into the room. "But I'll be back tomorrow."

"I don't want to be a nuisance," he told her, "but I'd like that very much."

"You could never be a nuisance. I'll be here every day until you can go home."

"What about your trip to Carmel? I don't want to interfere with that."

"I'll postpone it," she told him firmly, "until you are well enough to come along."

She knew one thing. She was going to look after him now, no matter what he said. He was no longer in any position to argue. He needed someone, and it was obvious that his grandson, famous writer or not, didn't have much time for the old man.

Oh, he was here now, Linnet thought scornfully, but that was only because Glenn was sick. Before that, he always seemed to be out of town and out of his grandfather's life.

"I don't want you to do that," Glenn was protesting feebly.

Linnet could see that he was growing tired.

"There's no rush," she said lightly. "If we can't go this weekend, we'll go next weekend. Now, if you need or want anything, just call me." She moved the books in his lap to the bedside table and picked up her pocketbook. "Or have a nurse call me." She leaned over and kissed him on the cheek. "Try to rest," she said softly. "I'll be back in the morning."

"Bring Brad and Joanna with you," he told her just before he closed his eyes.

"Wait for me in the hall," Jon said peremptorily as she tried to slip out the door while he and the doctor were still talking. "I'll say goodnight to Grandfather, then drive you home."

Linnet lingered in the hallway for a few moments. The tone of his voice had annoyed her. She didn't want him to drive her home. She didn't want to have to talk to him. She was suddenly furious with him for the way he had been ignoring his grandfather. The fact that he was well known and undoubtedly well off made it even worse. If that sports car he drove was any indication, he obviously had enough money to see to it that his grandfather didn't have to live in that run-down section of town near the portion of waterfront where they met each day. Jon could easily afford to take better care of his grandfather, and Linnet was afraid she would tell him so. The more she thought about Jonathan West, the angrier she became.

No, she decided, it would not be a good idea to ride home with him. With her high heels tapping briskly on the bare floor, she walked down to the nurses' station.

"I'd like to leave a message for Mr. West," she told the nurse on duty. "Would you tell him that Miss Brooks took a taxi home?"

The nurse nodded and made a note on a pad of paper in front of her. Linnet had almost reached the elevator when she heard her name.

"Linnet," Jon called in low tones. "Wait!"

He caught up with her at the elevator. "Where are you going? I said I'd take you home." Again his voice was peremptory, and again it annoyed her.

"I'm going to take a taxi," she said evenly. "I think you should stay here with your grandfather."

"My grandfather is sound asleep," Jon told her, "and the doctor says he should sleep through until morning. There is nothing I can do here. Besides, I'd like to talk to you," he said, refusing to admit to himself the real reason he wanted to see her home.

There was something in his voice Linnet didn't like. What could he want to talk to her about? Whatever it was, it was nothing compared to what she had to say to him. She abandoned her idea of a taxi. By forcing her hand, he had asked for what she was going to tell him.

"Good," she answered. "I'd like to talk to you too."

"Well, we can't talk here," Jon said, keeping his voice low.

Linnet followed his glance. The nurse was staring at them openly.

"She probably recognizes me," Jon said with some irritation. "This happens all the time."

"It's the price you pay for having your picture on the dust cover," Linnet told him a little too sweetly. She was still angry.

The nurse started coming toward them.

"She must want an autograph," Jon said. His irritation had changed to resignation. He began to search his pockets for a pen.

The nurse gave Jon an apologetic smile. "Excuse me for interrupting your conversation," she said before turning to Linnet. "Are you really Linnet Brooks?"

Linnet nodded. She didn't trust herself to speak. A fountain of laughter was welling up inside her. The look on Jon's face was priceless.

"I've read all your books," the nurse said excitedly. "I think they're wonderful. I love your heroines, and the heroes . . ."

She glanced over at Jon and Linnet could almost see what she was thinking. Jon did look like one of her heroes. He didn't act like one of them, though, Linnet told herself. Her heroes were warmer, more caring, than Jonathan West seemed to be.

"I even have one with me," the nurse was saying. She held up a copy of *Morning's Promise*. It had just been released. "Could I have your autograph? I've never met an author before."

"I'm glad that you enjoy my books," Linnet said. She took the book and pen from the nurse with a warm smile.

"You know," the nurse went on as Linnet inscribed a few lines in the front of the book, "working in intensive care can be pretty depressing sometimes. But no matter how bad the day has been, your books always give me a lift."

"And you've given me a lift just by telling me that," Linnet said as she closed the book and handed it back to the nurse.

"Thanks, Miss Brooks," the nurse said.

The elevator doors opened. With a final wave at the nurse, Linnet stepped inside. Jon followed and they rode down to the lobby in silence. As they walked through the darkened parking lot, Linnet was still trying not to laugh, though she was beginning to feel a little sorry for him too. That must have hurt his pride, she found herself thinking. He had been so sure the nurse had recognized him. Oh well, she thought as she remembered how irritated he had been, it will teach him not to take his readers for granted.

"How well do you know my grandfather?" Jon asked when they had finally reached his car and were on their way to her house.

Linnet's feeling of amusement evaporated. "Well enough to know that you've been neglecting him," she returned evenly.

It was late and she was suddenly aware of how tired she was and how worn out by the shock of seeing Glenn in the hospital attached to a variety of machines. She couldn't get his weary, white face out of her mind. As a result, her words were not as tactful as they might have been, as they should have been, she amended. Still, she wouldn't withdraw them.

"Neglecting him?" Jon asked with cold surprise. "How?"

"By letting him live in that seedy, run-down apartment, for one thing," Linnet told him. Anger was putting new life into her voice. "It's no wonder he had a heart attack. Do you know how hot it was on Tuesday? His apartment probably isn't even air-conditioned."

"Have you ever seen this apartment of his?" Jon asked. There was a note in his voice she didn't understand.

"No," Linnet replied. "He would never let me see it. I think he's ashamed of it. He's never even given me his phone number—probably because he's afraid I'd use it to find out where he lives."

Linnet looked over at him. He was staring straight ahead and his face was rigid with what Linnet assumed to be anger. For a moment she was sorry for the things she had said. Then Jon's face seemed to disappear and in its place, Linnet could see Glenn as he lay in the hospital bed suffering. She was no longer sorry for her outspokenness. These things needed to be said. What difference did it make whether they were said tonight or tomorrow? The important thing was to make Jon realize that his grandfather needed him.

"It's not as if you can't afford to do something for your grandfather," she said, controlling her anger. "It would be one thing if you didn't have the money. But you do have the money. It wouldn't hurt you to get him out of the city for the summer. He did raise you, after all, and I know he loves you very much. It's your turn to do something for him."

"How else do you think I'm neglecting him?" Jon demanded. "Go on, don't spare my feelings."

Linnet noted the sarcasm in his voice, but she ignored it.

"Since you asked, I think you should have made arrangements to spend his birthday with him. At his age, he shouldn't have to spend it with a virtual stranger."

He started to speak, but she wouldn't let him. She knew what he was going to say. It was a common enough excuse.

"I know you're busy," she told him. "Believe it or not, I know what kind of research your books entail. Nonetheless, you should make time for your grandfather. You're all he has, and he won't live much longer."

"Any more criticisms, or is the lecture over?"

He was obviously angry, and a part of Linnet didn't blame him. She had spoken frankly, more frankly than she would have done if she hadn't grown so fond of Glenn and if she hadn't been so emotionally drained by the shock of finding him in the hospital. She could only hope her words would start Jon thinking.

"I'm sure you can think of other ways you've been neglecting him," she replied. "You don't need me to tell you what they are. Your conscience can do that." She suddenly became aware of how prim she sounded, and she blushed slightly. At their worst, her heroines didn't sound as bad as that.

She looked around her, thinking they should have reached her house by now.

"You're going the wrong way," she protested. There was a note of panic in her voice that surprised her as much as it did him. "I don't know what you have in mind, but it's late and I'm tired. I want to go home."

"Relax," he said with a flash of amusement. "I'm not one of your heroes. I don't have anything in mind that you'd find the least bit compromising." His voice took on a sensual drawl. "Though under different circumstances . . ."

Linnet was shocked to find that she was almost disappointed. She must be more tired than she realized, she thought in horror. Surely she didn't want to touch him, didn't want him to touch her?

"I'm taking you to see where my grandfather lives," Jon told her in a voice that brooked no disagreement. His anger had returned. "I thought you would find it interesting, especially after everything you've had to say."

They were driving down a curving, tree-lined road. The large houses sat well back, sheltered from the noise of the cars by large trees and shrubs. Linnet knew this part of town. Geographically, it wasn't too far from her own. Financially, well paid though she was, it was as far removed as the moon. It certainly was unlike the run-down area where she had assumed Glenn lived. She glanced over at Jon but decided not to question him. There was a closed look to his face as he turned down a long, sweeping driveway. She was beginning to think she might have said too much.

"Surely Glenn doesn't live here!" she exclaimed as Jon stopped in front of a spacious, elegant-looking three-story home. Even in the dark, Linnet could see that the lawn was beautifully manicured and the garden was spilling over with carefully tended flowers.

Jon watched with grim amusement as Linnet stared at the darkened house in confusion.

"I thought he lived over near the waterfront."

"Did he ever tell you he lived there?" Jon asked.

"No, but . . ." Linnet floundered, ". . . but he was always so secretive about where he lived. I got the idea he was ashamed of it. And his clothes—" she rushed on, trying to justify herself. She was beginning to feel like a colossal fool. "They're always so shabby looking."

"I agree with that," Jon said. "I can't get him to buy any new ones. He says there's no point in buying anything new at his age."

He got out of the car.

"Would you like to see the inside?"

It wasn't a question, and she knew it. Jon had every intention of showing her just how wrong she was.

He ceremoniously ushered Linnet out of the car—a little too ceremoniously, she thought. Though he was still angry, she had the feeling that he was beginning to enjoy himself. She could hardly blame him, not after the things she had said.

She looked up at the imposing house. It made hers look positively insignificant.

"Does he live here alone?" she asked in awe as Jon opened the door and they stepped into a large hall.

"There's a chauffeur who lives in an apartment over the garage and . . ."

"A chauffeur?" Linnet interrupted. She was starting to feel a little bemused. Had she been completely wrong about the old man?

No, she thought, she hadn't been wrong about his loneliness. That was real and it had nothing to do with how much money he had.

"And there's also a housekeeper who lives here," Jon was saying.

"What about you?" Linnet asked. She was recovering from her surprise. "Where do you live?"

"I have a ranch in the mountains," Jon replied cautiously.

"Then you don't live here with your grandfather?" she asked, though she knew the answer. "He lives alone with only a housekeeper for company?"

She was glad to see Jon wince at that. She may have been wrong about Glenn's financial situation, but she wasn't wrong about his loneliness. He was a lonely old man, and that was Jon's fault.

"I've tried to get him to come live with me," he said

defensively, "but he won't. He says this is his home and this is where he's going to stay."

"I can understand that," Linnet murmured softly. "All his memories are bound up in this place."

Jon gave her a thoughtful look as he led her into the living room. Linnet walked around the beautifully furnished room, examining it with interest. On one wall was a Chardin; on another wall, a small Monet. A large bookcase held what appeared to be first editions.

No, she thought as she looked around her, Glenn wasn't the pensioner she had thought him to be. But why had he let her think he was?

"I don't understand," she said a little helplessly. "I don't understand any of this."

She hadn't meant Jon to overhear her, but he did. The anger in his face softened a little as he saw the bewilderment in her eyes.

"How long have you been meeting my grandfather?" he asked gently.

"For about three months," she answered.

"You don't know very much about him for someone who has been seeing him every day for the past three months," he observed, keeping his voice gentle.

"You're right," she confessed. "But I do know that he's a kind, decent man. I care for him very much."

Tears began to fill her eyes and she tried to blink them back, hoping Jon wouldn't notice. Seeing Glenn lying so defenseless in that bed had really upset her, she realized. What she needed was a good night's sleep.

Jon had seen her tears. In two strides he was beside her. He raised his hand and brushed them away with his finger. Linnet felt a tiny thrill as his finger touched her face. His anger seemed to have disappeared and, for the first time, Linnet could see some of his grandfather's kindness in his face. Perhaps he wasn't so bad after all, she thought, trying to be dispassionate, trying to ignore her sudden breathlessness.

Gently Jon drew her to him. She stood in the circle of his arms and rested her head on his chest gratefully. There was a gentleness about him that surprised her. Surprising or not, though, she found it comforting, and she was in the mood to be comforted. She felt a sudden urge to slip her arms around his neck and cling to him. She had actually made a move to raise her arms when she realized what she was doing. Shocked, she tried to step back, but Jon's arms were locked around her and she couldn't move. What was she thinking of? she asked herself sternly. If anyone was to do the comforting, it should be her, not Jon. She had known Glenn only a few months, but Jon had known him all his life. Undoubtedly he was more upset than she was. He just wasn't showing it.

"I'm sorry for the things I said earlier," she told him, leaning back in his arms. She was very much aware of the lower half of her body pressed against his, though she was trying to ignore it.

She studied his face carefully. Now that she looked closely, she thought she could see worry etched in the lines around his eyes. All at once she could tell that he was taking his grandfather's illness hard. She wondered how she had missed it before.

How she regretted her tactlessness. She had done nothing, absolutely nothing, to make it any easier for him.

"Why don't we sit down?" Jon suggested. "I think there are some things we should talk about."

He still didn't release her completely. It was almost as though he found solace in the closeness of her body. He moved toward the sofa, and Linnet took advantage of the movement to seat herself in a small chair flanking the fireplace. She sat down there purposely. She didn't want to be too close to Jon. That sudden surge of compassion she had felt, that desire to comfort him, had surprised and shocked her. From the look of him, he was certainly able to take care of himself and she doubted if he needed, or would even want, her sympathy. She would be wiser to think of herself, not him. Considering the way she had been behaving since she first saw him at the restaurant, she was going to need all the wisdom she could summon up.

Chapter Three

"Glenn didn't exactly lie to me," Linnet said, taking the initiative, "but he didn't tell me the truth either. He deliberately let me think he was just getting by. I'd like to know why."

"Knowing my grandfather," Jon said as he sat down in a chair across from her, "I'd guess it was because he wanted you to like him for himself. He may have thought that if he let you know about his money, you'd be more interested in that than in him."

Linnet was shocked and showed it. "How could he think that?"

"I'm sure he doesn't now. But it may have crossed his mind when he first met you. You're a beautiful young woman," Jon went on appreciatively.

His eyes touched her face, then her body, in a way Linnet had never experienced before. She wanted to squirm away from his gaze but she didn't. She forced herself to sit still.

"Not many young women like you would be willing to spend so much time with an old man. I must admit the thought that you were after his money crossed my mind," Jon added casually, "when he told me he had started meeting a young woman each morning."

Linnet looked at him indignantly. Two pink spots stained her cheeks.

"I don't know how you could even think such a thing. As if I would ever . . ."

"It's not so hard to believe. Think about it from my point of view. My eighty-five-year-old grandfather calls me one day and tells me that he's met a beautiful young woman, a young woman who reminds him of my grandmother."

Linnet looked startled and started to speak, but Jon held up a hand to stop her.

"He and my grandmother were very close, and it almost broke his heart when she died. So when he told me he had met someone who reminded him of her, I wasn't sure how to react. Since her death, he's been, well, vegetating, just waiting until it's his turn to go. But now that he's met you, all that has changed. He has something to look forward to each day."

Linnet got up and walked restlessly around the room.

"I had no idea," she murmured. "I knew he enjoyed meeting me, but I didn't realize the meetings were so important to him."

She was both shocked and touched. Shocked that he should have been so lonely and touched that she had been able to do something about his loneliness.

"Naturally," Jon went on, "I didn't want him to be hurt. So I didn't say much to him, other than to warn him to be careful about what he told you. If you were some kind of gold digger . . ."

"A gold digger!" Linnet exclaimed partly in horror and partly in amusement. Shades of the 1930s! "Gold digger" was such an outworn phrase that Linnet didn't even use it in her novels. "I would never . . ."

It was his turn to interrupt her. "So it would seem," he said a little dryly.

Linnet looked at him sharply. What did he mean by that? She was beginning to get a little angry.

"You can't blame me for wondering. Even though Grandfather claimed you knew nothing about him, you continued to meet him each day, something that I can't really explain—even now."

"I met him each day because I care for him, because he's the kind of person I would like to have had for a grandfather," Linnet told him coldly.

Her anger had grown until she was furious. Of all the things to be accused of, being a gold digger was one of the worst she could think of. Gold digger, she thought to herself. Where had he gotten that expression?

"There's no hidden motive for you to worry about and"—she waved a hand around her to encompass Glenn's house—"even if I had known about all this, there would still be no hidden motive for you to worry about. I'm not exactly poor, you know."

"That's another thing that worried me," Jon said. He looked as though he was beginning to enjoy himself.

Linnet wasn't enjoying herself at all. She looked at him suspiciously.

"I kept asking myself what kind of woman would be a romance writer. After all, romances aren't exactly great literature, and . . ."

Linnet knew where this line of thought was taking him. She had met this kind of man before.

"I might ask the same thing myself," she said, cutting off his words. "What kind of man buries himself in the past, researching and writing biographies of figures who have been written about over and over again? Or, for that matter, what kind of man would leave a dear old man like Glenn alone with only a housekeeper for company?''

She gave him an icy glance.

"Then, when Glenn does find someone who takes an interest in him, you decide to worry,'' she said scornfully. ''It seems to me that you should have been worrying about him years ago, not weeks ago.''

That made him angry. He stopped lounging in the chair and sat up ramrod straight.

"You don't know anything about my relationship with my grandfather.''

"Only what I see,'' she told him quietly. ''And I see a lonely old man with a grandson, his only family, who can't even be bothered to spend his birthday with him.'' She stood.

Jon got to his feet and towered over her. It was all Linnet could do to keep from taking a step backward. Looming over her as he was, he seemed incredibly big. Still, she held her ground.

"Not that it's any of your business,'' he said in clipped tones, ''but I had intended to spend Grandfather's birthday with him. It was only when he told me he had other plans that I decided to go out of town. How do you think I felt when he told me he'd rather spend his birthday with you?''

They stared at each other in silence. Linnet searched Jon's eyes, wondering if he was telling her the truth. What she saw there convinced her that he was. Behind the anger she had provoked was a kind of astonished hurt.

Again she regretted her tactlessness. She was definitely not at her best around him.

Jon, too, seemed to regret his outburst.

"Let's start again,'' he suggested. ''We're both upset about Grandfather, and I'm afraid that's causing us to say things we might not say otherwise.''

He took her arm and steered her toward the sofa. Linnet

found herself sitting next to him, close but not touching. She could smell his cologne; she could almost feel the warmth of his body. It unnerved her.

"I think I owe you an apology," she said a little unsteadily. She wasn't sure if the unsteadiness in her voice came from his closeness or the turmoil of her thoughts. All she knew was that she was terribly aware of him. "I was wrong about your neglecting Glenn financially, and perhaps I was wrong about your emotional neglect as well."

Their eyes met again and Linnet could see that the anger had disappeared from Jon's face. Now he merely looked tired, as tired as she felt.

She leaned back, wondering what she could do or say to banish the worry from his eyes. She should have seen it before, she told herself regretfully, but his sexuality had gotten in the way.

Gently, hesitantly, she laid a hand on his bare forearm. Beneath her fingers, she could feel his warm skin, textured by coarse dark hair. As she touched him, a chill slid down her back. There was something about him that loaded even a simple gesture like this with sexual significance.

"You're very worried about your grandfather, aren't you?" Her voice was soft.

"Not as worried as I was. But Tuesday night when he called me complaining of chest pains . . ." Jon's voice trailed off; then he began again. "He's all the family I have too."

He raised his eyes to hers, and Linnet saw a vulnerability she knew he usually kept hidden.

Why was he letting her see it, she wondered. Then she felt a rush of compassion, and she knew it didn't matter why.

"He'll be all right," she said, wanting desperately to banish the bleakness in his eyes.

Her hand slid slowly up his arm until she could pull him

close and cradle him in her arms. His head rested on her shoulder, just above her breast. Linnet wondered if he could hear the pounding of her heart.

"He's stronger than he looks," she said reassuringly.

"I hope so," Jon mumbled.

Linnet looked down and saw that his eyes were closed. He was exhausted. Slowly, rhythmically, she stroked his hair.

"When was the last time you slept?" she asked.

"I've spent the last two nights at the hospital," he confessed. "Tonight is the first night I felt comfortable leaving."

"You should go to bed," Linnet told him. "I can take a taxi home." She tried to get up but Jon's arms encircled her waist, keeping her in place.

"Not yet," he said. "Unless, of course, you'd like to join me in bed."

Linnet's heart all but stopped as she thought of the two of them in bed, their bodies pressed together in the darkness. Stop it, she told herself firmly. He hasn't even kissed you and you're imagining . . .

She managed a shaky laugh. "I don't think you've got the energy for that," she said teasingly. She didn't know what else to say.

This was a new situation for her. She'd been—what was the word for it—propositioned before. Those times, she'd had no difficulty in refusing the man, even dismissing him. She didn't want to dismiss Jon but, she thought a little confusedly, she didn't want to go to bed with him either.

"You're right. If I weren't so tired, I'd take advantage of this situation. Imagine lying in the arms of a beautiful woman and being too tired to do anything about it." He chuckled softly.

Though his words were regretful, Linnet thought she heard a note of contentment in his laugh. She was anything but content. His head had slid down until it rested just over her heart. Linnet could barely breathe. His body pressing against hers was playing havoc with her senses. She could smell nothing but soap and cologne mixed with a faint odor of manliness. She could feel nothing but the weight of his head on her breast and the strength of his arms around her waist.

"As much as I'm enjoying this," Jon said, finally lifting his head, "it's hardly fair to use you as a pillow, though you make a very soft one."

His eyes dropped briefly to her breasts in a glance that was something like a caress. Linnet was sure the color in her face had deepened.

Jon brushed his lips across hers lightly. Though their lips barely touched, Linnet's mouth felt scorched. Nervously she moistened her lips with her tongue. Jon watched her with narrowed eyes, then touched his lips to hers again. It was a gentle caress, like the last one, but Linnet felt it down to her toes.

"If I had more energy," he told her in a low tone, "I'd kiss you properly." This time the regret in his voice was real. "But there's no sense in starting something we can't finish."

Linnet's brain seemed frozen. She could think of no reply. Now was the time she should rebuff him, put him in his place. But she couldn't.

Jon reached up and slowly ran a finger over her lower lip.

"Such a kissable mouth," he muttered. "I wish . . ."

He sat up then and Linnet immediately pulled as far away from him as she could.

"How long have you lived here in Santa Barbara?" Jon asked. He raised his gaze from her lips to her eyes.

It was a question from out of the blue, and it took Linnet a moment to understand it. Obviously the kisses he had bestowed upon her hadn't affected him as they had her. For him they were just a way of passing the time. For her they were . . . she didn't want to think of what those kisses or the feel of his body meant to her.

"For about five years," she replied, surprised that her voice could sound so calm when her heart was beating a mile a minute.

"Then you're not a native Californian."

"No, why?"

"I was just wondering why you hadn't heard of my grandfather. He's quite well known around here. At least," he amended, "he used to be. The public has a short memory. Have you heard of Western Bank and Trust?"

"Of course. I have an account there." Who hadn't heard of it, she wondered. It was the largest bank in southern California.

"My great-grandfather founded it, but it didn't really come into its own until Grandfather took over. He's the one who made it what it is today." His words had a proud ring to them.

Linnet stared at him in surprise. This was an evening for surprises. First she had learned that Glenn's grandson was none other than *the* Jonathan Weston, and now she was discovering that Glenn was a personage in his own right. She was beginning to understand the flashes of imperiousness she had occasionally seen.

"I had no idea," she said for the second time that night.

"I can see that," he said. "It would seem that I owe you an apology too. You're obviously not the kind of person I expected you to be. I think it was hearing that you're a romance writer . . ."

"Let's not go into that," Linnet said hastily, "or we'll be arguing again. We're both tired and you, especially, need some sleep. I think it's time for me to go home."

He stood up and extended his hand. After a moment of hesitation, Linnet took it. Touching him didn't seem to do much for her peace of mind. She removed her hand from his as quickly as possible.

"You're right. We're both tired. We can talk about this tomorrow."

"There really isn't anything more to say, is there?" Linnet asked swiftly. "I know that you're not neglecting your grandfather, and you know that I'm not trying to worm my way into his affections for the sake of his money. What more can there be to discuss?"

She didn't want to get into this kind of emotional discussion with him again. From now on she wanted to keep her distance. The way she had responded to his pain and the comfort she had taken from standing in the circle of his arms confused her. She didn't want to be attracted to Jon West, physically or any other way.

"I'm sure we'll find plenty to talk about," he told her.

But the drive back to her house was accomplished in silence. Linnet was busy sorting through her emotions. Jon, too, seemed preoccupied. It wasn't until they had pulled into her driveway that he spoke.

"I'll pick you up around nine tomorrow morning."

She looked at him in surprise. "What for?"

"You're going to the hospital, aren't you?"

"Of course, but you don't need to take me. I can drive myself."

"Your car is parked near the restaurant. Had you forgotten that?"

She *had* forgotten it. "I can take a taxi," she said. "There's no reason for you to come here."

She didn't want him to stop by for her. As far as she was concerned, the less time she spent with him, the better.

He seemed to read her thoughts. "It's on the way," he said brusquely.

"All right," Linnet said, giving in. It was hardly worth

arguing over, and it would be easier to go with him than to wait for a taxi. "Thank you," she added belatedly, thinking she had probably sounded ungracious.

"There's one more thing," he said as she opened the door and started to get out of the car. "Who are Brad and Joanna?"

Linnet stared at him. Where had he heard of Brad and Joanna? Surely Glenn wouldn't have mentioned them, not to Jon, who found fiction writers, especially romance writers, beneath his notice.

"I heard Grandfather ask you to bring them to the hospital tomorrow. Who are they? Friends of yours?"

Linnet began to laugh softly.

"It's no laughing matter," he said coolly. "He doesn't need visitors. He needs rest and quiet."

"Brad and Joanna are characters in the book I'm working on," she explained, subduing her laughter.

Jon didn't seem to find anything humorous in her statement. In fact, he looked incredulous.

"From the way you two were talking, I thought they were real people."

"In a way they are. To me, anyway. Don't the people in your books seem real to you?"

As he considered her question, his long fingers rested lightly on the steering wheel. Linnet found herself staring at them. His hands were strong, yet she knew for a fact that they could be surprisingly gentle. Considering the way she reacted to him, that was something she'd be better off not knowing. She forced herself to look back at his face. He was staring straight ahead as he thought about her question.

"Well, I don't write fiction, of course."

Somehow he made it sound as though fiction were less than respectable. Linnet stiffened, not so much because of the words but because of the tone in which he had delivered them. She couldn't help reacting like that. His prejudice against fiction annoyed her, and the sneer in his voice annoyed her even more.

"No," he went on thoughtfully. He seemed totally unaware of the subtle insult he had managed to deliver and the effect it had on her. "I wouldn't say that I think of them as living, breathing people. To me, they're more abstract than that."

"I'm not surprised to hear you say that," Linnet said tartly. She was still nettled. "It shows in your work."

Jon gave her a startled look as she got out of the car; then he seemed to recover himself.

"I'll see you tomorrow morning at nine."

Before she could answer, he sped away. Linnet stood staring after the fading lights of his car in consternation. Whatever possessed her to say such a nasty thing about his writing? No matter what he said about fiction in general, about romances, she should never have allowed herself to respond in kind. There was something about him, she thought as she let herself in the front door, that brought out the worst in her.

At nine o'clock the next morning, Linnet was ready and waiting at a window overlooking the street. She didn't want Jon in her house. That would be admitting him into a part of her life, and she was determined not to do that. As soon as Jon pulled up in front of her house, she was out the door and walking briskly toward his car.

She was wearing a light green dress with a short matching jacket in case the air-conditioning at the hospital proved to be too cold for her. Glenn, she knew, preferred dresses to the slacks or shorts she usually wore, and she had dressed to please him.

He got out of the car to hold the passenger's door for her. His eyes never left her as she came down the sidewalk.

Much to her discomfort and annoyance, he didn't confine his gaze to her face. His eyes took in the rest of her too, from the thin gold bracelet on her wrist to the high-heeled sandals on her feet. He also noticed the curve of her waist and the swelling of her breasts and hips.

So annoyed was she by his scrutiny that she resolved then and there never again to let her heroines endure anything similar. His eyes were making her acutely aware of herself in a way she didn't like. They were also making the walk to the car interminable.

She looks so cool and unapproachable, Jon thought as he opened the door. Her icy green dress heightened that image. He wondered, as he had wondered several times since she had cradled his head to her breast, if she had the passion of one of her heroines. He had never read a romance—he never read fiction of any kind—but he had heard them discussed frequently. He knew the heroines were often passionate women—passionate, but also idealistic. He wondered what it would be like to make love to such a woman, to a woman who came alive at his touch and only his touch.

The light in his eyes dimmed slightly. There weren't any women like that—not these days when casual sex was a way of life. Besides, she couldn't be as innocent looking, as untouchable as she appeared. Not considering the kind of writing she did. . . .

In spite of that, he couldn't stop himself from imagining what it would be like to make love to her. She had a look of freshness that intrigued him.

By the time Linnet reached the car, her cheeks were pink. Jon noted the heightened color in her face with interest. So, he thought, she's not as poised as she pretends to be. That pleased him.

"Good morning," he said. Suddenly it was a very good

morning. He gestured toward the thin briefcase in her hand. "Brad and Joanna, I presume?"

Linnet smiled in spite of herself. She was relieved to find he wasn't angry with her. That final remark of hers the night before about the characters in his biographies had been totally unnecessary.

"May I?" Jon took the briefcase from her and dropped it behind the sports car's bucket seats.

As his hand brushed hers, Linnet jumped. It was as though she had come into contact with a very pleasant kind of electrical current. There was something special in his touch, Linnet told herself as she slid into the car. She had spent the better part of the past night denying that fact to herself. Now there was no way she could deny it. His touch had the power to jolt her.

Jon had felt it too. At least she thought he had. For a moment, there had seemed to be a flicker in his eyes. On second thought, though, she wasn't so sure. Jon was concentrating on his driving, apparently not thinking of her at all. His next words proved it.

"I talked to the doctor this morning, and he said Grandfather had a very good night."

"I'm glad to hear that," Linnet said fervently. "I barely slept myself for worrying about him."

And about you, she thought to herself. Like it or not, Jon had affected her and she didn't suppose it was simply because he looked like one of the heroes in her books. There had to be more to it than that.

"This isn't the way to the restaurant," she said suddenly. "I've got to pick up my car. It might be towed away if I don't."

"I thought you could leave it there today," Jon told her easily, "and we could pick it up tonight after we have dinner."

Linnet stared at him in dismay. She didn't want to have dinner with him at an intimate restaurant like the Chez Nous. She didn't want to have dinner with him anywhere.

"If that's a dinner invitation," she said coolly, "I'm afraid I'll have to refuse. I'd planned on spending the evening at the hospital."

"We'll go after visiting hours are over, of course," Jon said imperturbably. "I've already spoken to the owner of the restaurant, and he says it's perfectly all right if you leave your car in his lot all day."

"But I won't be dressed for dinner at a place like that," Linnet protested. She didn't like the way he had made these arrangements without consulting her. "And I'll be tired as well. I really don't think . . ."

"You have to have dinner. It might as well be with me. Besides," he added casually, "Grandfather asked me to take you to dinner. He said it would make up for last night."

"You don't need to make up for last night," Linnet said sharply. She stared out the window, annoyed with herself. She hadn't liked it when she had thought Jon wanted to have dinner with her, but she liked it even less now that she knew Glenn had aranged the evening.

If she didn't know better, she'd say she was behaving just like one of her heroines. She'd say she was attracted to Jonathan West and that was what was making her feel so contrary. But, of course, that was ridiculous. He wasn't the type of man to attract her, and she knew it.

"I know I don't need to make up for last night, but I'd like to. Besides, we have some things to discuss."

Linnet looked over at him. "I thought we had already discussed everything," she said a little wearily. "Surely there's nothing more."

"I meant your trip to Carmel. Grandfather told me that you asked him to go along."

"I did, and the invitation still stands. Of course, we'll have to wait until the doctor says he can travel, but after that I can see no reason why he couldn't go."

"That's what I want to talk to you about," Jon said mildly. "And dinner is as good a time as any. All right?"

Linnet hesitated. "All right," she finally agreed. At least it was a public place.

At the hospital, Linnet's arrival made a stir. The nurse in the intensive care unit had lost no time in telling people about her. On the way to Glenn's room, she autographed five more copies of her book for members of the hospital staff. Jon attracted curious, even covetous, glances as he stood aside and waited for her, but no one seemed to recognize him. Linnet would have felt sorry for him if it hadn't been for his snide remarks about fiction and fiction writers.

"You seem to be quite well known," he said a little stiffly as they finally stepped into the elevator.

"I have written sixteen romances," she said lightly. "A few people, at least, should recognize my name."

He stared at her in amazement. "You've written sixteen of those novels?"

As usual, there was a note in his voice that she didn't quite like.

"Yes, I have," she said quietly, "and I'm proud of each one of them."

"You're obviously very prolific. Haven't you ever wanted to write something more challenging?"

"You don't think there's any challenge in thinking up fresh plots with fresh characters three or four times a year?" she asked, keeping her voice light.

She didn't want him to see how much his words annoyed

her. Besides, there was no point in starting an argument on the elevator.

"You should try it. You'd soon learn just how challenging it can be."

She watched the floor indicator above the elevator door and gave a sigh of relief when they reached their floor. She had met other people who enjoyed criticizing romances, and generally they hadn't bothered her. She usually just laughed their words off. But Jon was different. He annoyed her.

Glenn, she was glad to see, looked much better. There was color in his face, and his eyes contained their familiar sparkle.

"How do you like my grandson now that you've finally met him?" he asked later in the day when Jon had left the room to talk to the doctor. "Isn't he everything I said he was?"

"He certainly is," Linnet said dryly, "and more."

"I knew you two would hit it off," Glenn told her with a satisfaction that bordered on smugness. "I understand he's taking you to dinner."

"Yes, he is, but don't get any ideas," Linnet warned him. "I haven't forgotten how you tried to get us together."

"Me?" Glenn was all innocence.

"You! He's only taking me to dinner because you asked him to and I'm only going because . . ."

"I didn't ask him to take you to dinner," Glenn interrupted. "It was his idea entirely. But I can't say I'm not delighted."

Linnet shook her head repressively, though her spirits soared. Jon wanted to take her to dinner after all. He had only used his grandfather because she kept refusing his invitations.

"One dinner does not a romance make," Linnet told

Glenn. "I want you to promise you won't try any match-making."

"I don't need to." His eyes twinkled up at her. "I've done my part. The rest is up to you and Jon."

Linnet could only look at him helplessly. He was incorrigible.

Chapter Four

"I'd like the stuffed shrimp, please," Linnet said to Jon.

They were at the Chez Nous, and Linnet was every bit as uncomfortable as she had thought she would be. The restaurant was dark and intimate; their table was undoubtedly the most romantic the restaurant had to offer.

It certainly was the smallest, Linnet thought. She and Jon sat squeezed together on a plush banquette against the wall, their shoulders and thighs touching in a fashion that Linnet found unnerving. Try though she did, relaxing was out of the question.

When they first sat down, she had attempted to slide away from him, but there was no place to go. She was in the corner and Jon, so large and solid, apparently had no intention of giving her any extra space. It was impossible to break the physical contact between them.

Jon, she noted, seemed to be enjoying the enforced intimacy of their table while she was trying not to be bothered by the feel of his leg against hers. She wasn't succeeding.

"Is that all you want?" Jon asked in surprise. "You should be hungrier than that. All you had for lunch was that small salad from the hospital cafeteria and, from the look of it, it couldn't have been very appetizing."

"That's all I want."

She was hungry, but she had a good reason for not telling him that. A dinner with several courses would last forever —at least the way his thigh and hers fit together would make it seem forever—while a dinner with one course would end more quickly.

"You have to eat more than that," Jon said firmly. "I insist."

"That's all I want," Linnet repeated more strongly.

Jon ingored her. With mounting irritation, she listened as he ordered for her: cracked crab cocktail, mushroom and endive salad, white asparagus with hollandaise and finally, the stuffed shrimp.

"I can't eat all that," she protested angrily.

He was being the masterful male, and she wasn't sure she liked it.

"I'll help you," he said simply. "I'm starved."

Her irritation faded and she had to smile at the tone of his voice. Suddenly he wasn't so much the masterful male as he was the hungry boy. The change disarmed her, but only for a moment.

She groaned to herself as he gave his own order to the waiter: sauteed scallops, salad, asparagus, abalone steak and a raspberry soufflé to follow. From the sound of it, they were going to be there all night.

If only they weren't pressed so tightly together, she thought, fuming silently. If only the maitre d' had given them another table.

She pulled herself up short. It wasn't the maitre d' she

should be angry with—or even Jon, though his obvious enjoyment of the way they were squeezed together did nothing to temper her annoyance. If she was angry with anyone, she should be angry with herself. It wasn't the maitre d's fault her heart did erratic flip-flops whenever Jon touched her.

It probably wasn't Jon's fault either, she conceded reluctantly. It was her fault. She, and no one else, was to blame for the fact that she couldn't sit there and enjoy her dinner.

What was there about him that caused her to react this way? she asked herself as she gazed at him resentfully. He and the wine steward were deep in conversation.

Never before had a man caused her to feel like this. She didn't like it. She definitely didn't like it. Why, all he had to do was shift slightly and she'd be in his arms . . . the place she wanted so desperately to be and so desperately *not* to be.

"What are you thinking?" Jon asked.

The wine steward had disappeared, and they were alone in their secluded, intimate part of the restaurant.

"I'm thinking that the table is too small, that I can hardly see in the darkness, and that we're crowded together like sardines," she told him crossly.

He laughed. "You should feel flattered. This is the most sought-after table in the restaurant. Most couples would give a week's salary to sit here."

"I can't imagine why. There's barely room for our plates."

"That's not why it's sought after," he said simply. "For a romance writer, you're singularly unromantic." His tone was gently teasing, but the look in his eyes was serious.

She thought he seemed slightly surprised by her attitude. What had he been expecting, she wondered a little wildly. Meaningful glances and intimate conversation?

"I wasn't aware that we were here for romance," she said coldly. "I thought we were here to discuss Glenn."

"And so we are."

His voice was now polite, his eyes thoughtful. What is making her so irritable? he asked himself. Ever since they had walked into the restaurant, she had been jumpy and nervous. True, she hadn't paid much attention to him during the day and, while he found that disconcerting, it was also understandable.

But last night . . . last night she had been warm and desirable in a way that was more than sexual. She had reached out to him, comforted him with a sureness of instinct that still surprised him. No other woman had been able to reach him as she had.

That was last night, and whatever had motivated her was gone. Now she was trying to build a barrier around herself. She was trying to keep herself aloof from him, and even though their surroundings made aloofness almost impossible, she was doing a good job of it. He wondered why. Last night he could have sworn she was attracted to him—as he was to her. Tonight was a different story.

"Jon, darling!" a voice trilled from halfway across the restaurant. "Whatever are you doing at that tiny, dark table?"

Linnet winced as several of the other diners turned to peer at them curiously. The evening was getting worse.

The voice belonged to a tall, ravishing blonde dressed in what could only have been a designer original, a very expensive designer original. Linnet recognized the look immediately.

"Hello, Mimi." There wasn't much enthusiasm in Jon's voice, though he rose and allowed her to kiss him.

Mimi, on the other hand, was obviously delighted to see Jon.

"And who is this?" she asked, giving Linnet an appraising look.

Her perfectly made-up eyes took in Linnet's green cotton dress—so right for the hospital and so wrong for the Chez Nous—and instantly registered their disapproval.

Jon made the introductions.

"Linnet Brooks?" Mimi asked.

Her high voice carried to most of the tables in the restaurant. Linnet's face grew warm. People were looking at them again.

"I seem to have heard that name before, though I can't imagine where." She cast another disdainful look at Linnet's dress. "Surely we haven't met."

"No," Linnet said, hovering between anger and laughter. "We haven't met."

"Linnet is a writer," Jon said.

"Really?" Mimi asked, as though she found that very hard to believe.

"She writes romances," Jon added.

Linnet shot him a sharp look. Was it her imagination or did he sound embarrassed by that fact?

"Perhaps that's where you've heard her name."

"No," Mimi said dismissively. She didn't seem the least bit aware of her rudeness. "I'm sure that's not it. You know I don't have time to read . . . except your books, of course, darling," she added hastily.

"Of course," he said politely.

"Where have you been keeping yourself? I haven't seen you in weeks."

As Mimi put a possessive hand on Jon's arm, Linnet felt a stab of jealousy. It was followed immediately by a stab of astonishment. Surely she couldn't be jealous? It was a ridiculous thought, and yet it did bother her in some rather primitive way to see them standing so close together.

She had to admit they made a striking couple. Both were

tall and striking. Both were head-turners. And Mimi's sophisticated banter seemed to be exactly the kind of conversation a man like Jon would enjoy. He was laughing at something she had said, and the smile she gave him in return was enough to raise the temperature of any man.

Linnet's spirits sank. As she sat pinned in her corner, virtually ignored by Jon and Mimi, she was suddenly beset by shyness. She felt gauche and unsure of herself, two things she considered herself *not* to be. She felt dowdy and plain in a way she never had before. It wasn't a pleasant feeling, and neither was the jealousy which, all at once, seemed to be eating away at her.

Why had Jon wanted to have dinner with her when he could have dinner with a gorgeous creature like Mimi? she asked herself miserably. She felt alone and forgotten in her dark corner of the restaurant as Jon and Mimi chatted. If she could have slipped away, she would have.

Then Linnet's sense of humor began to assert itself. Mimi had all the attributes, and more, of the other woman, the nemesis of several of Linnet's heroines. Mimi was fiction come to life. With the lift of her eyebrows and the swish of her expensive dress, she was making Linnet feel like one of her own heroines.

No, Linnet corrected herself, Mimi was making her feel worse than her heroines, for they always had a measure of self-confidence and poise to fall back on in these situations, while her own self-confidence and poise seemed to have evaporated completely. If this had been a scene in a book, Mimi's theatrics would have been almost humorous, Linnet thought ruefully. But in real life, they were anything but funny.

"There you are," a man's voice said. "I've been waiting out in front for you."

What next? Linnet groaned to herself. She looked up to see a short, balding man approach them. When he stopped at their table, Mimi immediately released her hold on Jon and slid her arm through his.

"I was on my way out when I saw Jon, and I just had to come over and say hello," she explained to the other man.

Linnet stared at them in fascination. He was obviously her date, yet he couldn't hold a candle to Jon. He was several inches shorter than Jon and about thirty pounds heavier. His clothes, none too good to begin with, were mussed and rumpled looking. Mimi, however, was looking at him as though he were the most fascinating man in the room. She had lost all interest in Jon, and the full battery of her charms was now directed at the other man.

"Hello, Martin," Jon said, seeming relieved to see him.

Martin, Linnet learned, was Mimi's husband. She would never have guessed they were married. They seemed so unsuited to one another. For the first time, Linnet noticed the gold band on Mimi's left hand. She wished she had seen it before.

She looked at them with even more interest. Martin was speaking, and Mimi was hanging on to his every word.

"Linnet Brooks?" he was asking. "I know of you, of course. You're the romance writer."

"Oh?" Jon said. "You've heard of her?"

He sounded so surprised that Linnet was annoyed.

"Of course I have. I've even read a couple of her books. It's my business to know about good writers."

"Martin is in the movie business," Jon explained.

"If you ever want to try your hand at screen writing, give me a call," Martin said to Linnet.

"I will," she answered absently.

She couldn't get over the way Mimi was looking at Martin. It was obvious that she adored him.

As they walked away, Linnet could hear Mimi dissecting her.

"Why do you suppose she's dressed in that dreadful

cotton frock? If she's as successful as you say, she should be able to afford something better than that. For a moment, I thought Jon was losing his touch.''

Again her voice carried through the small restaurant and again heads turned toward their table. Linnet shrank back into the darkness of her corner. She didn't know whether to laugh or cry.

"I'm sorry," Jon said ruefully as he sat down beside her. He seemed oblivious to the stares of the other diners. "Mimi takes some getting used to."

"She certainly is an interesting character," Linnet said with a heartfelt sigh of relief that Mimi had gone. "For a few moments I thought the two of you . . . were . . . might be . . ." She paused, not knowing how to go on. She wasn't even sure if she wanted to go on.

Jon, however, understood what she was trying to say. He laughed.

"No, Mimi and I have never been involved. That's just the way she is. She and Martin have been married for seven or eight years now, and she has never looked seriously at another man in that time. Martin is her whole world. Perhaps you noticed that."

"I did," Linnet confessed, "but I'm not quite sure why."

He shrugged. "Who knows what attracts two people?"

Who knows indeed! Linnet thought. She would love to know what there was about Jon that attracted her so; she would also like to know what there was about him that had caused that sudden, unwelcome surge of jealousy. Perhaps if she knew what it was, she could guard against it. She had to guard against it or, before she knew it, she'd be behaving just like one of her heroines.

"The doctor says Grandfather will be able to leave the hospital in a few days," Jon said.

They had finally finished all the food Jon had ordered,

even the raspberry soufflé, and were lingering over small cups of espresso. The food had mellowed Linnet slightly. She no longer sat so rigidly in the corner, trying to keep from all physical contact. She had reached the point where she was enjoying the contact between them.

Why not enjoy it, she told herself philosophically, since, short of demanding another table, there was nothing she could do about it?

"He'll still need a great deal of care," Jon went on, "but at least he won't have to stay in the hospital."

"That's wonderful," she replied. "I'm sure he'll be delighted."

"Of course he will be. The question is, what are we going to do with him?"

Linnet was subtly flattered by his use of the word "we." He seemed to be implying that she was now an important part of Glenn's life.

"I've really been worried about him," Jon confessed as his face clouded over.

"These last few days have been difficult," Linnet said. "I've been worried too."

"I know you have." Jon's face cleared, and he smiled at her warmly. "It's sweet of you to take such an interest in someone you've only known for a few months."

"He means a great deal to me," she said simply.

"And you mean a great deal to him." Jon slid his arm across the back of the banquette and rested it on her shoulders. "Now that I'm getting to know you, I'm beginning to understand why."

With his other hand, he lightly traced a course down her cheek, then tilted her head back so he could look at her.

Their eyes met for a long, breathless moment. As Linnet stared into his eyes, she could feel herself being drawn toward him. The warmth in his face was magnetic, and it pulled her closer and closer until she was afraid she would drown in the intensity of his gaze.

Her lips parted slightly. Without taking his eyes from hers, Jon ran his finger over her mouth, her upper lip first, then her lower lip. It was a simple caress, but Jon managed to load it with sexual meaning. Linnet saw the sensuality of it reflected in his eyes.

Without quite realizing what she was doing, she moistened her lips. Jon's eyes narrowed and left hers long enough to watch the movement of her tongue. Then his eyes returned to hers, and Linnet once more felt herself drowning in his gaze.

"If only we weren't in this damn restaurant," Jon said.

Though his voice was low, it was filled with frustration. He wanted to take her in his arms and kiss her. He wanted to kiss her gently, to kiss her passionately. He wanted to feel her lips part beneath his, he wanted to feel the warmth of her body as it molded itself to him.

He had to get her out of here, he thought with a surge of impatience. He wanted—no, he needed to take her some place they could be alone. He needed the pleasure and the release she could give him, and he wanted desperately to give her that same pleasure in return.

His words broke the spell of his gaze, and Linnet suddenly became aware of the clinking of glasses and silverware at the nearby tables. She became aware, too, of the fact that their lips were only a few inches apart.

In another second or two, Linnet thought, they would have been kissing in front of everyone in the restaurant. She sat up abruptly.

"We were talking about your grandfather," she said in a voice that was none too steady.

"My grandfather," Jon repeated mechanically.

He shifted slightly in his seat, hoping to relieve the

pressure their closeness had produced. He didn't want to talk about his grandfather at that moment. He wanted to make love to Linnet. There was only one thought in his mind and that was the thought of their bodies pressing together and becoming one.

With a sigh of regret, he pushed the thought to the back of his mind. Business first, he thought. After that, there was the whole night in front of them.

"He can go to Carmel with me," Linnet was saying. "I've just been waiting until I know when he can travel to make all the arrangements."

"I've got a better idea," Jon said. "I'm going to take him up to my ranch, and I'd like you to come up and stay also. Grandfather would be delighted to have you and, I have to admit, I would too." His eyes roamed over her face, investing his words with an unmistakable meaning.

"Your ranch?"

Linnet stared at him in shocked surprise. Every instinct she possessed cried out in protest. She couldn't live under the same roof as Jon. Only seconds before, she had come close to losing herself in his eyes. What would happen if they shared the same house?

Linnet shied from that thought nervously and rationalized her reaction to his suggestion. How, she asked herself, could she live under the same roof with a man who was openly scornful of her writing?

"Don't you see, it's the perfect solution," Jon told her.

"It's not the perfect solution!" she exclaimed.

"Why not?" He was taken aback by her vehemence.

A few moments ago, he could have sworn she wanted the same thing he did: to be together, to be able to love freely. Surely he couldn't have been wrong about something as basic as that.

Linnet had spoken without thinking. Now she had to clutch at straws in order to justify herself.

"You said yourself that Glenn has never before agreed to move up to the ranch. What makes you think he'll agree now?"

"Things are different now. Even Grandfather will have to admit that." Jon was confused, terribly confused. Why was she acting like this? What had gone wrong?

"That's no reason to bully him into moving up to the ranch if he doesn't want to go," Linnet said sharply. "Besides, he's already agreed to go to Carmel with me."

They couldn't stay at the ranch, she was thinking. The way she trembled when he touched her, even the sudden jealousy she had felt earlier, told her that. Living under the same roof with Jon would be madness.

He was looking at her curiously, so curiously that Linnet wondered if her fear was showing.

"What's so special about Carmel?" he wanted to know.

"The house I'm going to rent is quiet," she said, trying to think up reasons why she and Glenn should go to Carmel instead of the ranch. With her thoughts in such turmoil, it was difficult to do.

"It won't be as hot there as it is here," she went on. "Glenn will be able to do nothing but rest and recuperate."

"He can do that at the ranch," Jon pointed out, "just as easily as he can in Carmel. More easily, in fact. I'll hire a nurse . . ."

"I can hire a nurse for him myself," Linnet put in. "If you're worried about the kind of care he'll get while he's in Carmel with me, you needn't. I'll watch him very carefully. I don't want anything to happen to him any more than you do."

"If you come up to the ranch," Jon said persuasively, "you won't have that kind of responsibility."

"I don't mind the responsibility," she said stiffly.

"I know you don't, but there's no reason for you to have to take on something like this. Think of it this way. The ranch will provide a vacation for you too. You'll have plenty of free time to spend with Grandfather. You can even write if you want to.''

She was aware that he was doing his best to persuade her to move up to the ranch for a few weeks. He was determined to have her at the ranch, and she knew it was not simply for his grandfather's sake. The thought frightened her as much as it elated her. She wasn't sure she could resist him.

She shook her head. ''I don't know,'' she said slowly.

She was at a disadvantage. All of Jon's arguments made more sense than hers did. Still, her instincts told her that going to the ranch would be a mistake, perhaps the biggest mistake she had ever made.

''What do you have against going up to the ranch?'' Jon asked. He sensed that she was weakening. His eyes rested thoughtfully on her face

''It's not that I have anything against your ranch,'' she said. ''It's just that I've got a lot of work to do . . .''

''I thought Grandfather said you were taking a vacation,'' he interrupted.

''A working vacation,'' she amended. ''I have a deadline coming up, and my book is a little behind schedule as it is. I really need to be somewhere I can finish it.''

''Then my ranch is the perfect spot for you,'' he said triumphantly. ''You'll have all the time you need and none of the routine of housekeeping to distract you.''

She sighed. It wasn't the housework she was afraid would distract her. It was Jon.

''Perhaps you and Glenn could go up to the ranch and I could come for frequent visits,'' she said slowly. ''There really isn't any reason why I have to live there, is there?''

''There's a very good reason why you should stay at the ranch,'' Jon said crisply.

He was perplexed. It had never occurred to him that she

would put up so much resistance to the idea. Her resistance fired his determination to have her at the ranch where the two of them could spend long nights together. If they had been alone a few moments ago, he would have kissed her and caressed her and, in spite of the way she was acting now, she would have welcomed his touch. He was sure of it.

"I don't think Grandfather will agree to move up there unless you come too."

He pushed his espresso aside and leaned toward her. He was so close that Linnet could feel his breath. She stared down at the table.

"Grandfather can't live in that big house by himself anymore," Jon said firmly. "I've got to get him up to the ranch where I can see that he's looked after properly."

Linnet nodded. "I can understand that. But . . ."

Jon was beginning to lose patience. Why couldn't she see how important this was—to his grandfather and to himself. He wanted Linnet more than he had ever wanted a woman. What's more, he didn't want her for a few brief hours. He wanted a longer, more intense relationship. He knew his longing for her couldn't be assuaged by a night or two in bed. He wanted to get to know her mentally as well as physically, and the ranch was the ideal spot for that.

He took a deep breath and tried to sound reasonable.

"I've already told you how much he thinks of you. I'm afraid he'll insist on staying in the city so he can continue these daily meetings of yours. But if you agree to move up to the ranch with him now, he'll be perfectly content."

"That's all very well and good," Linnet said tartly. "But I can't stay at your ranch forever."

"Not forever, but long enough to ease the transition. It's going to be very difficult for him to leave his home no matter when he does it. It will be a little easier for him if he goes now and if he has you to help him."

Linnet was losing ground and she knew it. All of Jon's arguments made perfect sense to her.

Again, Jon sensed that she was weakening. He put his hand over hers, hoping to recreate some of the intimacy they had felt earlier.

"I'd like you to come up to the ranch too," he told her. "For my sake as well as Grandfather's."

A little unwillingly, Linnet glanced up. The look on his face nearly stopped her heart.

"You'll like the ranch," he went on. "After living in the city, you won't believe how quiet it is. It's so secluded and private that you can wander for miles without seeing anyone."

Normally that would have sounded like heaven to Linnet. Now, though, with her hand in Jon's, it filled her with apprehension. His next words justified that feeling.

"We can lose ourselves in the woods," he told her softly. "No one will be able to see us, no one will even know where we are."

Linnet didn't answer.

"I have horses, so you can go riding if you wish," he continued, "and there's a small swimming hole filled with beautifully clear water where we can swim when it's hot."

"I haven't said I'd come," she said as she pulled her hand from his grasp. Jon was making the ranch sound inviting, too inviting. "I want to talk to Glenn first and see what he really wants to do."

Jon felt a moment of pure exasperation. He shrugged. "I was just trying to point out some of the advantages of the ranch," he said, suddenly sounding indifferent. He had no intention of begging her to come, no matter how much he wanted her. He motioned to the waiter for the check. "Are you ready to leave?"

"Yes."

She wanted to add that she had been ready for an hour,

but she knew that wasn't strictly true. As the evening had worn on, Linnet had begun to enjoy herself. She had found herself talking to Jon quite comfortably, even flirting a little now and then. It was only when he suggested that she move up to his ranch that she had panicked.

And with good cause, she told herself. This evening had shown her how vulnerable she was to him . . . as if last night hadn't been proof enough.

She hurried out of the restaurant ahead of Jon and got into her car quickly, before he could think of another reason why she should leave it there overnight. She wasn't going to let him take her home. He would probably want to come in, and once inside . . .

"Thank you for dinner," she said politely as she rolled down her window slightly.

"Perhaps I should drive you home," Jon said. He looked at his watch worriedly. "I had no idea it was so late."

"I'll be fine," she told him firmly.

Jon looked at her doubtfully, and for a moment Linnet thought he was going to insist on taking her home. She started her engine.

"All right, but lock your doors," he told her. "I'll see you tomorrow at the hospital."

Linnet nodded and sped away. Once she was out of the restaurant parking lot, she rolled down her window completely and let in the balmy night air. She wished it could clear all thoughts of Jon from her mind as easily as it cleared the stuffy air from the car. She wished she knew what to do.

Jon had put her in a ridiculous position by insisting that Glenn would move up to the ranch only if she agreed to go along. Now, if she refused to go, as common sense told her she should, Glenn would be the one to suffer. Linnet knew she couldn't do that to him. She would far rather go up to the ranch and face Jon each day than be responsible for hurting Glenn.

She adjusted her rear-view mirror slightly. The lights of the car behind her were shining into it and creating a glare. She slowed down a little as she moved the mirror around. The other car slowed down too.

Was it following her? she wondered with a flash of fear.

She turned suddenly onto a side road, and the car behind her turned also. Linnet drove around the block, and by the time she was back on the thoroughfare she was sure she was being followed. Considering the hour and the deserted streets, it was a frightening thought. She forced herself to be calm and started looking for an all-night gas station or drug store—anywhere there would be people. She certainly wasn't going to lead whoever was behind her to her dark, empty house.

She came to a stop light and sat waiting for it to turn green, nervously drumming her fingers on the steering wheel. As the other car coasted to a stop behind her, she forced herself to look into her rear view mirror again. This time, thanks to the street lights, she could see the driver of the car clearly. It was Jon!

Fear gave way to relief and then anger. Why was he following her? What right had he to frighten her like that? she fumed as she pulled into her driveway. She got out of her car and stalked over to his sleek sports car.

"Why were you following me?" she demanded angrily. She still hadn't gotten over the scare he had given her.

"I was following you to see that you got home safely," he said coolly. He hadn't expected this kind of a reaction.

"Oh." Linnet felt deflated and a little foolish. "I thought . . ."

"You thought I expected some kind of payment for the dinner," he finished for her. Now it was his turn to sound angry. "The men in your books may act that way, but it's not my style. I followed you simply because it's not safe for a woman to be on the road by herself at this hour."

"Thank you," Linnet said quietly. There was nothing else she could say. She was touched by his thoughtfulness, his concern for her safety.

"You're welcome." Jon grinned suddenly, and his anger disappeared. "Of course, if you'd like to show your gratitude with a kiss, I won't object." His eyes went suggestively to her mouth.

Linnet was tempted; more tempted than she cared to admit. After all, what was one kiss? Surely there couldn't be any harm in one kiss.

Jon reached out and touched her arm, though he made no attempt to pull her toward him. His eyes were still on her mouth. Linnet shivered.

Slowly, as though she wasn't sure she was doing the right thing, she leaned over. Her lips touched his lightly in a kiss that was really a teasing caress.

It wasn't enough for Jon. He wrapped his hand around the nape of her neck and held her mouth against his. This time their kiss was longer and more satisfying. Linnet kissed him back, completely mindless of the fact that they were kissing under the bright light of the street lamp.

When she finally pulled away, she felt a little dazed and her breath was uneven. Now she knew what harm there was in one kiss. One kiss led to another. If she didn't take care, those kisses could lead to something more than she could handle.

Chapter Five

"I think Jon's right," Glenn said.

He was propped up against several pillows. Though his color was better, his voice was far from strong.

"As much as I'd like to spend some time with you in Carmel, I'm afraid I'd be too much trouble. The doctor tells me I'm going to have to take it easy from now on, and I don't want to be a burden to you."

"You wouldn't be a burden to me," Linnet protested. "You'd never be that."

Glenn took one of her hands in his own. Linnet looked down and absently noted how the blue veins stood out. His skin was nearly transparent and it reminded her how weak he was.

"That's nice of you to say," he told her softly, "and I know you mean it. But the fact remains that I'm something of an invalid and I'm not likely ever to be anything else. At

Jon's ranch I can have a nurse, and my doctor will be only an hour or two away.''

It was obvious his mind was made up. There was nothing Linnet could say that would change it.

Jon was behind all this, she thought with exasperation. Though she had gotten to the hospital early that morning, it hadn't been early enough. Jon had already been there, and he had persuaded his grandfather that the ranch was the ideal place for him to recuperate.

"Besides," the old man said, "Jon said you had agreed to stay with us at the ranch. As far as I can see, everything is working out perfectly. You'll get your vacation, and I'll get to have you near me without feeling that I'm a burden.''

Linnet gave up trying to convince Glenn that he would be better off in Carmel. In her heart, she knew Jon was right. The ranch was the best place for Glenn. It just wasn't the best place for her.

"Jon did suggest that I stay at the ranch for a few weeks," she said uncomfortably. "But I don't really think it's such a good idea.''

Glenn looked surprised. "I understood it was all settled.'' There was a question in his voice.

"Not really. I gave it a great deal of thought last night,'' Linnet went on hurriedly. That was true. She had thought of nothing else. "It will be very difficult for me to move all my things up there; my typewriter, my research notes and, of course, there will be calls to and from my editor.''

"You'd have to move all those things to Carmel," Glenn pointed out reasonably. "And you were willing to do that. As for the telephone calls, Jon has a telephone. I'm sure he won't mind your using it whenever you want.''

Even to Linnet, her excuses sounded lame. But what else was she to say? There was no way she could explain her reaction to Jon, especially to his grandfather. Glenn would never understand. She barely understood it herself.

"I won't exactly be the ideal guest, you know. I have a deadline to meet, which means I'll have to spend hours working."

"And the ranch is the perfect place for that," Glenn said, just as Jon had. "You won't have to do anything but work and spend a little time with me. Jon has a wonderful housekeeper who's used to the peculiarities of writers. I'd venture to say that Jon is a far more temperamental writer than you are," he added shrewdly. "So you needn't worry about inconveniencing anyone."

"In that case, he might not like having another writer in the house," Linnet told him. Particularly a romance writer, she added to herself. His better-than-thou attitude toward fiction writers was one of the things holding her back.

"Nonsense. He wants you to come as much as I do." Glenn's eyes grew troubled. "I think there's something you're not telling me. Don't you like Jon?"

"Of course I do," she said quickly.

She wasn't about to tell this dear, kind old man that she didn't like his grandson. Besides, she did like him. Sometimes she liked him too much.

"You know," Glenn said with a dignity that touched her deeply, "I might not live much longer."

"Don't talk like that," Linnet told him robustly. "The doctor says you have years in front of you, if you take care of yourself."

He waved away the doctor's opinion with his hand. "What do doctors know?" He leaned back and contrived to look as frail and weak as he could. "It would mean a great deal to me to have you at the ranch, for a few weeks at least."

"This is emotional blackmail," Linnet said accusingly. She didn't know whether to be annoyed or amused. Glenn was determined to get what he wanted. "You know perfectly well that you're going to be fine. You're only using your illness to get your own way."

There was a twinkle in Glenn's eyes that he couldn't quite hide. "Humor me," he urged her. "I'm an old man and I deserve to be indulged."

Linnet laughed. "All right," she said, capitulating suddenly. She couldn't resist him any longer. "I'll come."

Perhaps she was making a mountain out of a molehill, she thought to herself as she listened to Glenn talk about the ranch. She hoped so.

Three days later, Glenn was discharged from the hospital. Linnet picked him up and took him directly to the ranch. Jon had already moved Glenn's things and arranged for a nurse to be on duty when they arrived.

While Glenn directed her to Jon's ranch, Linnet marveled at the beautiful scenery. She had never driven through the Santa Ynez Mountains before.

Jon's ranch was perched on the side of a hill overlooking the Santa Ynez Valley. The valley was only forty-five minutes from Santa Barbara, but it seemed to Linnet that she had entered another world. Some of the rolling hills were lush and green, some were covered with scrubby shrubs, others were clad in golden grasses.

Finally, she turned down the road that led to the ranch. A few moments later, they pulled up in front of what once had been a working ranch house but had obviously been modernized.

Large windows looked out over the tree-covered mountains, and a long deck ran along the entire side of the house overlooking the valley. There was a stable that housed both cars and horses; above it was what looked to Linnet like a self-contained apartment.

"This is quite a setup," she commented to Glenn. "It's not exactly what I expected."

But then, she reflected, nothing about either of the West men was what she expected.

"When Jon said he had a ranch, I pictured something a little more rustic."

"Jon has done quite a bit to it, of course," Glenn told her. "He loves the seclusion and privacy he has up here, but he likes his comforts too."

They had just come to a stop when Jon hurried out the door, across the wide covered porch, and down the three steps to Linnet's car. Obviously he had been watching for them.

Just behind him came a small, rotund woman who was hastily drying her hands on a towel looped through her apron. Behind her came a bustling, motherly looking woman in a starchy white uniform, who pushed a wheelchair down the makeshift ramp that spanned the stairs.

They made quite a reception committee, Linnet thought. She got out of the car and stretched.

"Welcome," Jon said, giving Linnet a warm smile.

The smile reminded Linnet that she had to be on her guard around him. She gave him an impersonal smile in return, which he didn't see. He was helping his grandfather out of the car and into the wheelchair.

"I don't need this thing," Glenn objected. "I'm perfectly capable of getting into the house on my own."

"It's only for a few days," the nurse said soothingly, "while you get your strength back. I'm Betty Richards," she said before Jon had a chance to introduce her. "You just call me Betty."

She gave Linnet a shy smile.

"It's such a thrill for me to be working in the same house with you," she said. "Mr. West told me that you're Linnet Brooks, the romance writer."

"I've read your books too," chimed in the other woman. "I think they're just wonderful."

"Romance groupies," Jon said. "I'm surrounded by romance groupies."

Linnet shot a quick look at him, but he seemed more amused than anything else.

"This is Rachel Johnson," he said to Linnet. "When she isn't reading your books, she's my housekeeper."

Linnet thought there was a slight sting to those words, but Mrs. Johnson didn't seem to notice. She gave Jon an indulgent smile, then turned her attention to Glenn.

"You look a little peaky," she said as the nurse began wheeling him into the house. "That will be the hospital food. I can see I'm going to have to feed you up."

Alone with Jon, Linnet felt nervous. What was there about him that made her so nervous? It was a question that had vexed her from the first moment she had laid eyes on him. He made her heart beat more quickly; he made her body glow with an unexpected warmth, and she didn't like it. However, the irritation she felt did nothing to settle the butterflies suddenly fluttering around in her stomach.

"It's beautiful up here," she said, gesturing around her. She gazed at the stable, the hills, the house—anywhere but into his eyes. "It's so peaceful and quiet."

"That's one of the reasons I like it so much," he told her.

As she listened to the trill of the birds, Linnet could easily understand the contentment in his voice.

"I'll show you around tomorrow, if you like. But right now, I think I'd better see that Grandfather has everything he needs. I'm sure you'd like to see your room."

"Yes, I would." The butterflies in her stomach were beginning to quiet down a little.

There was nothing to be nervous about, she told herself as she opened the back door of her car and pulled out a portable typewriter. Jon was being a good host and nothing more. If she could keep her own feelings under control, everything would be fine.

At that moment, Jon took the typewriter from her, his fingers brushing her hand as he did so. From the look on his face, Linnet had the feeling the caress was deliberate. Deliberate or not, it started the butterflies fluttering again.

She looked up at him, and the warmth in his eyes made her catch her breath. The look on his face confused her. She was sure he couldn't feel the same attraction for her that she felt for him, considering how little respect he had for her work. In an intellectual like Jon, respect and love would have to go hand in hand. Without respect, there could be no love, and Jon definitely did not respect her work and, hence, could not respect her.

All this flashed through her mind in the brief seconds it had taken him to transfer the typewriter from her hand to his, in the few brief seconds she had stared into his eyes.

Considerably shaken, she let him lead her into the house. Love! Whatever had put that into her mind? Surely she wasn't falling in love with him.

No, she answered herself firmly. She was not falling in love with him. She wasn't one of her heroines; she had more sense than to fall in love with a man who could offer her nothing but scorn and heartache.

"What do you think?" Jon asked a little shyly as they entered the house.

Beyond the wide hall was a large living room with huge, tall windows looking out over the valley. It was a beautiful room, with clean lines and a simple design. The wall opposite the windows was completely covered by built-in bookcases, and in those bookcases were rows and rows of books. Even Linnet, whose eclectic collection of books threatened to overflow her house, was startled by the number of books Jon had.

Against a third wall was a huge stone fireplace with a large hearth. Grouped around it were big, overstuffed chairs. The fourth wall, opposite the fireplace, held a collection of Western art. It was a comfortable, lived-in room, and it appealed to Linnet immediately.

"I like it," she said. "Very much."

Jon looked pleased. "I was hoping you would," he told her.

He raised his hand as if to touch her and, as he did so, Linnet moved quickly toward the bookcase where she carefully studied the titles. Jon's hand dropped back to his side, and for a moment he studied her as intently as she was studying the books.

"Grandfather's room is down the hall," he said finally. "I thought he should be here rather than upstairs. It will be easier for him to get around that way. The nurse will be right next door. If you're ready, I'll show you your room."

Linnet abandoned the bookcase and together they mounted the wide stairs opposite the door to the living room.

"What about Mrs. Johnson?" Linnet asked.

"She and her husband Hank live in the apartment over the stable. Her husband helps me around the ranch," he added. "He looks after the horses and cattle and generally helps with what needs to be done—chopping wood, mending fences, that kind of thing."

"You have cattle?" Linnet asked in surprise.

Jon grinned. "Not cattle, exactly. A few steers to keep the freezer stocked and some cows for milk. Rachel has a garden too, so most of our fruits and vegetables are home-grown."

Linnet looked at him curiously. "For some reason, I had the idea that this wasn't a working ranch."

"It isn't really—at least, we don't try to make a profit. But I like to be as self-sufficient as possible." He caught a glimpse of her face. "Why are you so surprised?"

"It's just that I've never pictured you doing that kind of work," she admitted slowly. She was impressed in spite of herself. She had always imagined him in his library, surrounded by books and research notes. Linnet glanced at his broad shoulders. Certainly they seemed to prove that he worked outside frequently. As for the rest of his body . . .

"The ivory-tower intellectual?" Jon said, guessing her thoughts. "It would seem that you still have some mistaken ideas about me."

"Just as I'm sure you still have some mistaken ideas about me," she retorted quickly.

"Do I?" he asked with a wicked gleam in his eyes. "I doubt it. This is your room," he added before she had a chance to respond.

Linnet's bedroom was small but comfortable. There was a sunny yellow bedspread on the bed, and the walls were lightly sprinkled with yellow flowers. Simple white curtains hung at the windows, and woven rag rugs covered the shiny wood floor. Linnet looked at the room appreciatively. It had an air of belonging to the ranch.

"You have your own bathroom," Jon said, "and my room is just next door."

"Next door?" she asked a little suspiciously.

That meant they would be upstairs alone every night. Linnet frowned. She would have been happier if his room was on the first floor with Glenn. She would have been happier still if he slept out in the stable.

"I thought that would be convenient, in case . . ." His eyes scanned her face.

"In case what?" Linnet asked coldly.

"In case you need or want anything in the night," he finished.

"I don't think that's very likely," she told him, keeping her voice icy. "As a matter of fact, I go to sleep early and I don't like being disturbed." She wanted him to understand there and then that she had come to the ranch for Glenn's sake. She had not come to provide him with any evening entertainment.

"That's too bad," he said. "Up here, the nights are the most beautiful part of each day. If you'd let me, I could show you things that would take your breath away." He slowly put down the typewriter and cupped her chin with his hand.

His words were spoken lightly, but the meaning in his eyes was clear.

Or was it? Linnet wondered breathlessly. Perhaps it was just her imagination that was giving his words two meanings. Imagination and wishful thinking.

Wishful thinking! She caught herself up short. She was becoming as fanciful as her heroines. They were always imagining what it would be like to be kissed by the hero, and now here she was, doing the same thing. She turned away from him as a faint flush of pink stained her cheeks.

"You'd better go see to your grandfather," she said in a dismissive voice.

"Perhaps I should." His eyes went to her cheeks for a moment.

When his eyes returned to hers, Linnet expected to see satisfaction in them. She expected him to be pleased by the fact that he had unnerved and embarrassed her. Instead she saw surprise, surprise and curiosity. That confused her. What had she done to surprise him?

"Dinner is at eight," he said as he moved toward the door. "I like to watch the sunset while I eat. Hank should be up any moment with your luggage."

He left then, and Linnet breathed a sigh of relief. Having him in her bedroom made her distinctly uneasy.

Chapter Six

For dinner, Linnet put on a conservative two-piece dress of aqua silk that was anything but sexy or provocative. She looked ladylike and altogether proper, she thought as she went in search of Glenn.

Much to her surprise, she found him in bed. Her heart sank. That meant she'd be alone with Jon for what was sure to be a romantic dinner watching the sunset.

"Aren't you eating with us?" she asked.

"I thought so, but it seems Betty has other ideas," he said ruefully. "If she has her way, I'll be asleep before you reach the main course."

"Now, Mr. West," Betty said reproachfully. "You know it's not me. Doctor's orders," she explained to Linnet. "He musn't overdo, you know."

"I'm sure you and Jon won't miss me," Glenn told her with a twinkle in his eye. "I imagine you two have a great deal to talk about."

"Yes, indeed," Betty inserted. "The two of you being writers, and all."

Linnet couldn't help smiling. She could imagine how Jon would react if he heard Betty put the two of them in the same category.

"Why don't I have my dinner on a tray in here with you?" she suggested suddenly.

As far as she was concerned, that would be an ideal solution. She would get to spend time with Glenn, something she always enjoyed, and she wouldn't have to face Jon alone over a romantic dinner. She remembered all too well their evening at the Chez Nous and how she had felt as they sat shoulder to shoulder, thigh to thigh, in the darkened restaurant. It was not an experience she cared to repeat.

"I wouldn't think of such a thing," Glenn told her firmly. "I want you to relax and have a proper meal. You've spent so much time at the hospital the past few days that I'm sure you haven't been taking care of yourself. Besides, Betty and I are going to play cards, and then I'm going to sleep."

"If you're sure—" Linnet said doubtfully.

She suspected that Glenn was trying to throw her together with Jon as much as possible. She wouldn't have put it past him to talk Betty into saying he had to go to bed early just so that she and Jon would be alone together. He was a matchmaker at heart. And Betty, she judged, was just as bad. Nothing would delight her more than the idea that she was furthering a romance.

"I'm sure," Glenn said firmly. "You enjoy your dinner and don't worry about me."

With that Linnet had to be content.

Jon was waiting for her in the living room. His eyes lit up appreciatively when he saw her.

"You are lovely," he told her. "And you grow more lovely each time I see you."

Linnet was surprised by the compliment, but she could tell it was sincere. If my work didn't stand between us, she thought with a stab of dismay, perhaps . . .

She pushed that thought away. Her work did stand between them. Silly as it might seem to some, Jon's disapproval created a barrier she couldn't surmount no matter how attracted she was to him.

He handed her a glass of white wine, and she accepted it silently.

"A friend of mine has a winery not too far from here," he said. "This is one of his wines." He opened the door leading to the deck and motioned to her to precede him.

"I didn't know there were any wineries in this area," Linnet said.

"There aren't many, and what few there are aren't very well known. Napa Valley, up north, gets all the publicity. Miguel's vineyard has been in his family for centuries, and he's improving the wine yearly. I should take you there for a tour. It's fascinating to see all the work he's done."

"I'm sure it is," Linnet told him quietly, "but I'm not here to sightsee. Perhaps once Glenn is better I might be interested. But until then, I'd like to stay close to the ranch."

What she didn't tell him was that once Glenn was better, she would be on her way back to her house in town.

She crossed the deck and slowly sipped her wine as she stared out over the valley below. Even with the sun gliding out of sight, it was a breathtaking vista, and the serenity of it began to affect her. She forgot Jon, forgot the turmoil he created in her mind, as she drank in the scenery.

She turned to find him standing beside her, looking down with the same puzzled expression on his face that she had seen earlier. What did he find so puzzling? she wondered.

"There's something about you," he began. Gently his finger brushed her cheek. "Something I don't understand."

Linnet forced herself to look into his eyes.

"I don't know what that could be," she said breathlessly. "I'm not a complicated person."

"You are to me."

His hand moved to her hair, and he stroked it slowly. His caresses were light and, from another man, would have been meaningless. From Jon, though, they were anything but that. Linnet felt the heat of his hand—she even felt the warmth of his body as he took a step closer to her.

"What don't you understand?" Her voice was little more than a whisper. In a protective gesture, she raised her wine glass and held it in front of her.

"I'll show you." Deftly, Jon took the wine glass from her hand and set it on the rail.

Linnet was expecting him to take her in his arms, and she had just started to turn from him when his voice stopped her.

"Don't run away," he commanded softly. "Look at me."

Reluctantly, she raised her eyes to his. Jon waited until their eyes made contact; then, with tantalizing slowness, he leaned forward and kissed her lightly. It was a gentle kiss, but it made Linnet's heart pound.

With his hands still at his sides, Jon kissed her a second time. This time, their lips seemed to cling together. Though only their lips were touching, Linnet could feel the kiss in every part of her body.

With the same slowness, Jon pulled away and Linnet opened her eyes to find him watching her.

"That's what I don't understand," he said a little unsteadily. The kiss had affected him as much as it had her.

Linnet stared at him blankly. She had no idea what he was talking about.

"I don't know . . ." she began.

Jon looked past her. "Here's our dinner," he said in a voice that suddenly sounded normal.

Linnet looked around to see Mrs. Johnson wheeling out a cart stacked with covered dishes of food.

"Let me help," she said immediately.

"I wouldn't think of it," the housekeeper said indignantly. "You're a guest here."

"I'd still like to help," Linnet told her. "Having three extra people in the house must be making a lot of work for you."

"To tell you the truth," Mrs. Johnson said with a fond smile at Jon, "I'm glad to have the company. I get tired of cooking for one. What Mr. West needs," she said confidentially, but not so confidentially that Jon couldn't hear, "is a wife and children. Then we'd all be happy—especially old Mr. West."

"You don't know anything about it, Rachel," Jon said indulgently.

Linnet didn't feel nearly so indulgent. She was wondering if Rachel, too, was interested in promoting a romance between Jon and herself. It certainly seemed as though everywhere she turned, romance was in the air.

She looked carefully at Rachel's open face and decided that she was letting her imagination run away with her. Love and marriage were her stock in trade and because she was attracted—sexually attracted, she told herself firmly—to Jon, she was unconsciously allowing thoughts about them to intrude into her personal life.

She sat down in the chair Jon held for her and concentrated on the dinner. It was delicious. Mrs. Johnson had prepared a savory stuffed tenderloin of beef, which was cooked to perfection. With it she served wild rice and peas straight from the garden. Jon poured out generous glasses of a dry red wine, which Linnet enjoyed more than she would have imagined. In fact, she was enjoying the entire evening more than she would have imagined.

"I'm surprised you didn't go into banking," she said when they had run out of small talk. "It certainly would have been a natural for you."

"You're right about that." He gave her a rueful smile. "In fact, my name was already on the office door when I decided to try my hand at writing. Grandfather all but disinherited me," he added in a joking tone.

Linnet saw beneath the attempt at humor. "That must have been difficult for you," she said gently. "Disappointing your grandfather couldn't have been easy."

Jon gave her a grateful glance. "It was difficult. Though he tried not to show it, Grandfather was very hurt. For years he had been talking about the two of us working together. He's the only father I've ever known, and I hated to let him down like that, but . . ." He stopped suddenly.

"You had to go your own way," Linnet finished for him.

He gave her a surprised look, as though he hadn't expected her to understand. She had abandoned her dinner and was staring at him through the gathering darkness. Their eyes caught and held for a moment before Jon went on. Something in her face seemed to give him confidence.

"It would have been easy for me to go into banking," he confessed. "Too easy. It would have seemed like cheating. I would have been the heir apparent and everyone would have known it. There would have been no challenge."

Linnet nodded thoughtfully.

"I wanted to prove something to myself. I wanted to make my own success, not step into someone else's," he said. There was a trace of defiance in his voice.

"That takes a great deal of courage," Linnet told him. "Striking out on your own is always difficult. In a case like yours, I'm sure it was doubly difficult."

"My friends told me I was every kind of a fool," he went on bitterly, "for giving up a soft job and cushy lifestyle. I lost most of them when I moved up here. That was before I was well known, of course," he added cynically.

"Then they weren't really your friends," Linnet said promptly. "You didn't lose much."

"You're right about that. They were interested in my name, not me." He fell silent.

"What happened after that?" Linnet asked.

She had pushed away her plate and was leaning forward with her elbows resting on the table and the bowl of her wine glass cupped in her hands. She didn't drink the wine, however. She was much too interested in what Jon was saying.

"Fortunately, I had a little money of my own. I bought this place, moved up here and immersed myself in history. When my first book didn't sell, I was so discouraged I almost gave up writing. Grandfather offered me another job at the bank, and I seriously thought about taking it. But it was too late. I couldn't do it. By that time, writing had hooked me."

"And now you're a success," Linnet said lightly.

He smiled somberly. "Hardly. Oh, critically my books are a success. But there's more to writing than that. I don't reach people the way you do."

Linnet didn't know what to say to that. He was right.

"Sometimes I wonder if I did the right thing," he mused. "I nearly broke Grandfather's heart when I turned my back on banking—and for what? For books nobody reads."

Linnet was swept by a desire to comfort him. He sounded so desolate. This was a side of Jon she had never imagined existed.

"That's not true," she said warmly. "Your books are read, by intelligent and interested people. They may not zoom to the top of the best-seller list, but they're not designed for that.''

"What do you think of my books?" he asked as though he really cared what she thought.

"I think your deductions and conclusions are often brilliant," she told him firmly. She was finding it hard to believe that she was reassuring Jonathan Weston, the critics' darling. "And I enjoy your writing style. It's very readable; it's clear, precise, and economical."

She didn't tell him that she occasionally found his treatment of the characters in his books wooden and ponderous. Now was not the time for that.

Jon looked pleased at her comments.

"I happen to know," she went on, "that your grandfather is extremely proud of you."

"I hope so," Jon said. "I've never wanted to let him down."

"And you haven't." She paused and looked at him thoughtfully. "But you know, Jon, it isn't what I think, or even what your grandfather thinks, that's important. It's what you think." She made her voice gentle. "Are you proud of the work you do? Does it satisfy something deep inside you?"

There was dawning respect in his eyes as he looked back at her. He searched her face for a long moment before he answered.

"Yes," he said finally. "I'm proud of what I do. It isn't perfect, of course, but I'm proud of my work."

"Then you're a success," she said softly, "in the most fundamental and important way of all."

He laughed, and there was a faint sound of triumph in his voice. "I've never thought of it that way," he told her. "But you're right, of course."

They sat staring across the table at each other, communicating wordlessly, until Linnet forced her eyes from his. Their gaze was growing a little too intense.

"Look," she said suddenly.

Unnoticed by the two of them, the sun had slipped behind the mountains on the other side of the valley, leaving the sky streaked with fiery pink.

"We almost missed it."

She stared up at the color-splashed sky, thinking more of Jon than of the sunset. He had shown her a vulnerability that surprised her. Surprising or not, she liked him for it.

As she watched the pink fade slowly from the sky, Jon watched her. He was as surprised as she was by the way he had opened himself to her. What is there about her? he asked himself. Without realizing it, he was echoing her thoughts of him. What is there about her that makes me want to take her in my arms and kiss her? What is there about her that affects me this way? She's been here only a few hours, but she looks as though she belongs here, as though the ranch is as much her home as it is mine.

Ever since Linnet had arrived, Jon had had the feeling that the ranch was now complete. He had never noticed any lack in his home before, but Linnet's presence added something special.

His mood changed abruptly, and he sneered inwardly as he realized how ridiculous, how corny, his thoughts were. Any minute now, he'd be sounding like one of the heroes in her books. He'd be better off sticking to facts. He didn't want to complicate his life with emotions and vague romantic notions. Linnet was a woman, just like any other, and nothing more. To consider her anything else was absurd.

"Would you like to go for a walk?" he asked. He got to his feet and held her chair for her.

"I'm a little tired," she said. She had the feeling she had

spent enough time with Jon for one evening. "I think I'll just go to bed."

"Nonsense," Jon said. "You can't go to bed after eating a meal like this. It isn't good for the digestion." He took her arm and helped her out of her chair. "A short walk will do you good."

The domineering male, Linnet thought as he led her down the deck stairs and off toward the stable. She had used him several times in her books. There were times when he came in handy. But this, she thought as she gently removed his hand from her arm, wasn't one of them.

Tactically, her move to free herself was a mistake. Instead of holding her arm, Jon simply put his own arm around her shoulders.

"It's a beautiful night," he said before she could protest at the way he was holding her close. "Look at that moon."

With his free hand, he pointed up at the large, round silver ball that was beginning to glow in the sky.

"I ordered it just for you. I wanted you to see how beautiful the ranch can be at night. All the familiar daytime shapes take on new forms," he went on quietly. "In the dark, the woods seem enchanted."

Linnet was surprised by Jon's sudden flight of fancy. She wouldn't have expected it of him. She was tempted to walk off into the dark with him. This side of him charmed her, and she wanted to see more of it. It was obvious that he had a hidden streak of the poet in him.

Then reality asserted itself and she stopped walking.

"I would really rather go inside," she said firmly.

She moved out of the circle of his arm. Tempted though she might be, she wasn't going to indulge in a bit of lovemaking in the moonlight, and the sooner he realized that, the better. For lovemaking was undoubtedly what he had in mind.

His face, what she could see of it in the moonlight, was suddenly boyishly appealing.

"Are you sure you'd rather go in? I was going to take you to one of my favorite spots on the ranch."

She hesitated. Some of Jon's mood was beginning to rub off on her. The night *was* beginning to seem enchanted. Jon noticed her hesitation.

"It's a small glen surrounded by towering pine trees," he told her. "It's beautiful in the daytime, but at night it becomes almost magical. Come with me. Please."

For Linnet, the enchantment of the night was growing and with it, the attraction she felt for Jon.

"We won't be able to see anything in the dark," she objected as she tried to be practical.

"No, but we can hear the wind rustling in the trees. We can smell the clean scent of pine, and we can see the stars overhead. It isn't far," he urged her. "I promise you'll be glad you went."

Linnet laughed and, as her laughter floated on the gently moving mountain air, she realized that Glenn would be delighted by the way things were going between them. She'd be delighted too, if it weren't for the nagging thought at the back of her mind that told her nothing had changed between them. Jon still didn't respect her work or her. No matter how magical the night seemed, that hadn't changed.

She thrust the thought from her. It wasn't a night for being practical. She could be practical tomorrow.

"All right," she said. "I'll go with you."

Hand in hand, they walked past the stable and into the woods. Only the moon and stars illuminated the path they were following. Linnet looked around her, but all she could see were the shadowy figures of the trees swaying ever so slightly in the summer breeze. Without Jon, she would have been hopelessly lost. She was grateful for the fact that her hand rested in his. Then, all at once, they were standing in a small clearing.

"Here we are," Jon said in a hushed voice.

"It is magical," Linnet told him softly. "We're only a few minutes from the house and yet there are no lights to be seen, no sign that civilization is anywhere near."

Above them the moon shone brightly, giving the grass and the trees a silvery cast. The only sounds to be heard were the sighing of the trees and the occasional chirping of crickets.

"Doesn't it give you the feeling that we're alone in the world?" Jon asked. "I come here whenever I've reached a difficult point in my work or whenever I'm fed up with the world or myself. I've never brought anyone else here. But you seem to belong to the ranch, somehow. Though you've been here just a few hours, you seem to be a part of it."

His own words surprised him. Only a few moments earlier he had dismissed such thoughts as ridiculously sentimental. Yet here he was, saying them to her.

Linnet's spirits soared. Perhaps she was wrong about the differences that stood between them, she thought joyfully. Perhaps they could be overcome.

"I'm glad I came," she said softly. "This place tells me a little about you."

He turned her so that she faced him. Very gently he caressed her cheek with his hand. Linnet tried not to tremble beneath his touch.

"Do you like what it tells you?" he asked.

She paused, then decided to tell the truth. It seemed to be a night for throwing caution to the wind.

"Very much," she replied.

His hand slid downward, then curved around the nape of her neck. He pulled her toward him.

Gently his lips touched hers. Linnet leaned against him,

feeling the strength in his arms as he held her. She felt her insides melt as the warmth of his body was transmitted to hers.

Jon raised his head, then pulled her down onto the soft, smooth grass. Linnet lay in his arms, looking up at him. Lazily she sketched the planes of his face with her finger. She had never felt so happy, never imagined such happiness could exist. Certainly when she had imagined the happiness of her heroines, it had never been anything like this. She felt as though she glowed with a radiance that matched that of the moon.

Jon seemed to think so too.

"You've never been more beautiful than you are now," he said quietly. Then his voice lightened. "I think I could see you with curlers in your hair and cream all over your face and I'd still find you beautiful," he said, teasing her gently.

Linnet laughed softly. "Oh no, you wouldn't. You'd run the other way."

"Don't you believe it. I'd never run from you."

He leaned over and lightly kissed her forehead, her cheeks, and the tip of her nose before his lips claimed hers again. This was a more possessive kiss, a deeper kiss, that started Linnet's blood racing. Her arms encircled his neck and she held him close.

"You have no idea how long I've waited for this moment," he told her.

She smiled up at him. "I've been waiting too," she heard her voice say.

The words shocked her, though she knew they were true.

Jon suddenly looked serious, and in the moonlight she could see that he was studying her.

She's so innocent looking, he was thinking. How much does she know of the passion she writes about? She can't know much, he answered himself, or she wouldn't be lying here with that trusting look on her face as she looks up at me. She doesn't seem to know the power of passion or what it can drive men to do.

Again he kissed her, but it was a tender kiss this time. When his lips reluctantly relinquished hers, he pulled her to her feet.

"It's getting late," he said. "Though I wouldn't mind spending the night here with you, I think we'd better go in."

"I suppose you're right," Linnet said. She didn't particularly want to go in either. They had shared a closeness that delighted her, and she was sorry to see it end.

"There will be other nights." The tone of Jon's voice turned the words into a promise.

Linnet blushed and started to turn away as she realized what he was thinking. He was going much too quickly for her, she thought, much too quickly. She had merely been savoring the feel of his arms and lips and the happiness she felt in his presence.

Jon's thoughts had progressed much farther. He was determined that there would be other nights. He wanted to discover how much she knew of the physical side of love, how much she knew of passion. And he had every intention of finding out.

Gently he turned her back toward him, then held out his hand. After a moment, Linnet put her hand in his and they walked back to the house together.

Chapter Seven

I acted like a fool, Linnet thought unhappily the next morning.

She was furious with herself for going off into the woods with Jon, furious with herself for listening to the things he had to say, furious with herself for letting him kiss her.

Thinking about it did nothing to calm Linnet down. She knew that a few kisses were hardly worth getting upset over—normally. But nothing about her relationship with Jon was normal.

I was worse than a fool, she repeated silently.

How could she have believed the things he had said? In the cold light of day, it was obvious that each word he uttered was part of his technique for wooing and winning women.

"You're so beautiful," he had said.

Without the moonlight to lend magic to his voice, Linnet

realized how corny the words were, and how insincere. She couldn't even give him credit for originality.

Now, she had to let him know that she didn't want to repeat last night. She had to convince him that there would be nothing more than those few kisses.

Her feet dragged as she went downstairs to breakfast.

"Good morning," Jon said. He rose as soon as he saw her and gave her a warm smile.

Linnet smiled coolly in return, though the welcoming look in his eyes did much to undermine her decision to keep her distance.

Jon held her chair and Linnet slipped into it, being careful not to let him touch her.

She drank her orange juice in silence and then began eating the eggs Jon had dished out for her from a covered dish on the table. Every mouthful was an effort. Linnet was more aware of Jon than she had ever been before.

Last night had done that for her, she thought bitterly. Now she didn't smell the coffee he was drinking or the ham on his plate. She smelled the odor of the soap and expensive cologne that clung to him. Now she couldn't concentrate on the spectacular scenery in front of her. His face got in the way. A few kisses had done all that, she thought angrily. Her own heroines weren't that silly. Could it be that she had fallen in love?

"What are your plans for the day?" he asked.

"I want to see Glenn before I make any plans," she answered briefly.

"I saw him just before breakfast," Jon told her. "He had a very good night."

"I'm glad to hear that." Linnet's voice thawed a little as she spoke. "I was afraid the drive from the hospital, plus getting settled in here, might have been a little too much for him."

"I was afraid so too, but the nurse seems to have him well in hand. She said he could spend some time out here on the deck after breakfast; then he has to rest for most of the afternoon. He might be able to get up for an hour or so later this afternoon, depending on how he feels."

"That sounds sensible," Linnet commented. She took another bite of her eggs.

"While he's resting this afternoon," Jon said, "I thought you and I could go horseback riding. There are some beautiful spots here on the ranch."

"If I'm not with Glenn, I'll have to do some work on my book," Linnet said. "I have a deadline to meet," she added, "so I won't have time for much of anything else."

The light in Jon's eyes faded, but Linnet didn't see it. She was staring miserably down at her plate of eggs, wishing things could be different between Jon and her.

There was a silence that stretched out until it began to get on Linnet's nerves.

"Is that the newspaper?" she asked in desperation.

She wanted to leave the table but, with her breakfast only half eaten, she was afraid that would look too much as though she were running from him.

Why didn't he leave? she wondered irritably. He was finished. There was no reason for him to sit there silently.

Wordlessly he handed it to her and, with a sigh of relief, Linnet hid behind it. Her eyes focused on the words, though they meant nothing to her. She wasn't at all interested in the news. She just didn't want to look up and see Jon staring at her.

Jon *was* staring at her.

I've been acting like a fool, he told himself bitterly. Last night, Linnet had been so gentle, so innocent and trusting. At least that was what he had thought at the time. Now he was beginning to wonder whether that was an act. How could she have been so approachable last night and so unapproachable this morning?

An unpleasant thought suddenly occurred to him. Had she been using him for book material? She had to get the ideas for her love scenes somewhere, he thought angrily. Perhaps that was what she was doing—trying out a scene for the book she was working on.

One thing was for certain: she hadn't been sincere. Her coolness this morning proved that. She was acting as though last night had never happened. Feeling an anger he didn't fully understand, Jon got to his feet and left the table without another word.

Once she was alone, Linnet mechanically folded the newspaper. She looked down at her eggs in disgust, then got up from the table herself. She'd go see how Glenn was doing, she decided.

He was sitting in his wheelchair with a blanket across his knees when Linnet reached his room.

"You're just in time to wheel me outside," he said as Linnet bent to kiss him.

Linnet looked doubtfully at the blanket on his lap.

"Won't you be a little too warm?" she asked. "It isn't as hot here as it is in Santa Barbara, but it's still on the warm side."

He grimaced comically. "This is Betty's idea," he said, gesturing toward the blanket. "Of course I'll be too hot. But I didn't have the heart to tell her that. She seems to feel that bundling people up makes them feel better. I'll take it off when we get outside."

Linnet smiled to herself as she wheeled Glenn down the hall and through the living room to the deck. Imagine Glenn sweltering under a blanket in the middle of June simply because he didn't want to hurt the nurse's feelings. If only Jon were that considerate of other people, she thought a little unfairly.

"There's something I particularly want to talk to you about," Glenn said once they were outside in the bright sunshine and Linnet had placed the heavy blanket on an empty chair.

"What it is?" she asked with some alarm. Glenn sounded so serious.

"For several years, Jon has wanted to do a biography of me," he said.

"That's wonderful!" Linnet exclaimed. Her alarm evaporated. "I'm sure he'll do an excellent job."

He held up a hand to stop her. "I haven't agreed to it yet. You see, there's one thing that's holding me back."

He glanced at Linnet and saw the look of surprise on her face.

"Don't get me wrong," he hastened to add. "I think Jon is a wonderful writer, and I enjoy his books very much. I'm very proud of him. But it seems to me that he often overlooks the human element when he writes. He ignores emotions and feelings in favor of cold, hard facts, and often cold, hard facts just aren't enough. Do you know what I mean?"

Linnet nodded thoughtfully. She certainly did know what he meant. This was her own criticism of Jon's work. Much as she enjoyed reading his carefully thought-out analytical theories, it frequently seemed as though some spark was missing from his writing.

"I've often wondered it if had anything to do with the fact that he lost his parents when he was so young," Glenn mused. "Amy and I tried to make it up to him, but I don't suppose anything could really make up for that kind of a loss."

Linnet didn't like the worried look on Glenn's face.

"Jon couldn't have had better grandparents, or even parents, than the two of you," she told him, meaning every word. "And he knows it too."

Glenn smiled at her gratefully.

"Perhaps," he said. "But I didn't really mean to go off on a tangent like that. I was telling you about the book he wants to write and why I've been reluctant to let him go ahead."

He fell silent, and Linnet did not prompt him. She waited for him to find the words he wanted to use. She knew it couldn't be easy for him to talk about Jon this way. With Amy gone, Jon was, quite simply, the light of his life.

"Jon has never understood the role love played in my life," he said finally. "He equates love with sex and, while they can go hand in hand, they often don't. He doesn't seem to realize that there is . . ." he paused, searching for a word, ". . . a spiritual side to love as well. I could never have been the success I was, or even the person I am today, if it hadn't been for Amy standing behind me, believing in me, encouraging me when things went wrong."

He gave Linnet a smile.

"I realize that sounds pretty old-fashioned these days, but I still believe that in a happy marriage, the husband and wife complement each other. I like to think that I gave Amy as much as she gave me."

"I'm sure you did," Linnet said softly.

Tears had filled her eyes. That was the kind of love she had always dreamed of for herself, the kind of love she wrote about. Would she ever find it?

"I've never been able to make Jon understand that," Glenn went on. "Whenever I try to explain, he listens politely, but I can tell he's just humoring me. I've been afraid that in any book he wrote about me, he would minimize or ignore the role Amy played in my life, and that would be neither fair nor truthful. That's why I haven't agreed to this biography—until now."

"Until now?" Linnet echoed. "What made you change your mind?"

He reached over and patted her hand. "You did, my dear," he said.

"I did?" Linnet was genuinely surprised. "How?"

"After I had known you for a few weeks, it occurred to me that you might be able to teach Jon things about love that I hadn't been able to."

Linnet blushed, hoping Glenn wouldn't notice. There was nothing she'd like more than to teach Jon about the kind of love she and Glenn believed in, but she doubted that it could be done. Last night, during those few magical moments, she might have believed she could do it, but not this morning. This morning, common sense told her that the scorn Jon felt for her would keep him from learning anything she could teach, just as it would keep the two of them from sharing anything.

"You're attractive, kind, compassionate," Glenn told her, "and you're intelligent. As soon as I met you, I knew Jon couldn't help but admire you."

Linnet wished Glenn were right, but the only thing Jon seemed to admire about her was her ability to bring him temporary contentment of a physical kind—and any woman could do that. Certainly, he didn't seem to admire her intelligence.

"I'm afraid you're wrong," Linnet said as calmly and matter-of-factly as she could. "Jon doesn't admire me. If anything, he looks down on me for writing romance. He seems to think it isn't worth reading or writing."

Glenn's eyes twinkled. "He'll come around," he said imperturbably.

"I doubt that."

"Wait and see," Glenn advised. "In the meantime, I want you and Jon to collaborate on my biography."

"Collaborate!" Linnet sat up straight and burst out laughing. As if Jon would work with her! "Jon will never agree to collaborate. I've just finished telling you how contemptuous he is of my work. He would never agree to let me help with one of his books.'' And I'm not sure I'd want to, she added to herself.

Uncannily, Glenn seemed to be following her thoughts.

''What do you think about the idea?'' he asked. ''Would you be willing to work with Jon?''

Linnet thought of the derogatory things Jon had to say about the kind of work she did. She thought of the way he attracted her, almost against her better judgement. She thought of the way she felt when he kissed her, of how she had gone off with him last night when she had known better.

No, she wasn't willing to work with him day in and day out for the length of time it would take to write a book of that nature, not as long as Jon attracted her as much as he did. And certainly not as long as he considered the creators of romance to be second-class writers. However, one look at Glenn's eager face told her that she couldn't say these things to him.

''Of course I'd like to work with Jon,'' she said, picking her words carefully, ''especially on something as special as your biography. I just don't see how I can. I have a book to finish by the end of the summer and a contract for two more.''

Glenn's face was a study in disappointment, and it upset Linnet to see it. Goodness knew, she thought with a little spurt of anger, she didn't want to be the one to hurt him.

''Couldn't you juggle your work assignments some-how?'' he asked. ''There must be some way you could do both. It would mean so much to me at my time of life,'' he added, letting his voice trail off.

Linnet looked at him suspiciously, wondering if he was trying to use his illness to manipulate her. His face, however, showed nothing but his disappointment. Her little spurt of anger grew. Why should she be the one to disappoint him? It certainly wouldn't hurt anyone if she agreed to collaborate with Jon, she reasoned. She knew very well that Jon would never go along with Glenn's plan.

"Well," she said slowly, "I suppose I could talk to my editor and see if there's some way I could do both."

Instantly the disappointment on Glenn's face was replaced with eagerness.

"That would be wonderful!" he exclaimed. "Do you really think you could work it out?"

"I can try," she said with a smile, knowing there would be no need for her to work it out. Jon would never agree. "I don't want you to get your hopes up, though," she said, making her voice gentle. "It isn't my cooperation you need, it's Jon's."

"Oh, he'll agree," Glenn said blithely. "I'm sure of that."

Linnet smiled and said no more. There was no sense pouring cold water on Glenn's plans. Jon could do that. For if there was one thing of which she was fully confident, it was Jon's reaction to Glenn's suggestion that they collaborate.

"Absolutely not," Jon said in a voice that was ominously calm.

The three of them were having lunch on the broad deck overlooking the valley. Glenn had put his proposition tactfully to Jon, but Jon, as Linnet had predicted, rejected it immediately. He didn't even bother to think about it.

"I don't need to collaborate with anyone," he went on coldly. "Least of all someone who . . ." he paused, ". . . who has no experience in the kind of writing I do."

Linnet looked at him sharply. She knew what he had wanted to say. He had wanted to say that he had no intention of collaborating with someone who did the kind of writing she did. Consideration for his grandfather had obviously kept him from saying what he really meant.

Though she had predicted Jon's reaction, Linnet found she was a little angry. She was wondering whether she should leave the table and let them argue it out between them when Jon beat her to it. He got to his feet as Glenn was speaking.

"I know you don't need to work with anyone," Glenn was saying. "But I thought you'd enjoy working with Linnet. She may not have written a biography before, but there's no reason she can't do a good job. She is a very good writer."

"She's a romance writer," Jon said, as though she weren't there. Now the contempt in his voice was plain. "I'm sorry, Grandfather, but I won't work with someone whose idea of a book is a series of love scenes. Not even for you." He flung down his napkin and stalked out of the room.

As Linnet watched him go, regret took the place of anger. The last thing she wanted was to be the cause of an argument between Glenn and Jon. Glenn meant too much to her for that—and so did Jon, said a tiny voice in her head. Linnet pushed that thought aside and turned to Glenn with a rueful smile.

"I was afraid he'd react that way," she told him.

Glenn, however, was still eating placidly. He didn't seem nearly as upset as she had thought he would be.

"He'll get over it," he told her. "Once he's had time to think over what I told him, he'll realize I'm right. You'll see."

Linnet doubted it, but she said no more. Glenn was the one who would see.

After Betty came to claim Glenn, Linnet spent most of the afternoon in her room, trying to work on Brad and Joanna. She had decided to stay out of Jon's way. Consider-

ing his anger when he left the table at lunch, there was no
telling what he would say if he saw her.

The writing was tough going. She kept seeing Jon's face
when she should have seen Brad's, and each time Brad
touched Joanna, Linnet imagined that Jon was touching her.
When there was finally a knock at the door, she welcomed
the interruption.

"Come in," she called, thinking it was Mrs. Johnson or,
perhaps, Betty.

Instead, it was Jon who opened the door. Linnet felt a
flicker of surprise, but it disappeared almost immediately.
In her books, unlikely scenes were always taking place in
the bedroom. Why shouldn't that happen in real life?
Surprise was replaced by unease. Scenes played within a
few steps of the bed usually ended up in a passionate kiss,
Linnet recalled. She felt her pulse leap wildly. Would that
happen here? No, she answered herself firmly as she
realized what she was thinking. She wouldn't allow it.

Not that it was likely, she thought as she noticed the
anger in Jon's face. Jon hadn't come to her bedroom for
kisses but for harsh words. Linnet pushed her chair away
from the small desk, stood, and faced him across the room.

"I want to talk to you," he said.

The harshness of his voice hurt her, though it didn't
particularly come as a surprise.

"Very well," she said calmly. "I'd ask you to sit down
but, as you can see, there's only one chair."

And that one chair she was now using for support. The
anger in the craggy contours of Jon's face was a terrible
thing to see.

"Perhaps we should go into the living room."

"We don't need to go into the living room," he said
curtly. "What I have to say won't take long."

"Very well," Linnet said again, waiting for him to
begin.

His mouth was tightly compressed and his body was rigid. She searched his face carefully. It was granite hard. For a brief moment, she thought she saw a kind of hurt behind the anger. Compassion flooded over her. Of course he was hurt. He saw his grandfather's proposal as a rejection of his work. Linnet suddenly wanted to take him in her arms and comfort him.

"What are you trying to do?" Jon was asking angrily. "For years I've been trying to interest Grandfather in this project and he has always refused. Now you come along and he's suddenly willing, but only if I'll let you collaborate with me. How did you manage to talk him into that?"

"I didn't talk him into anything," Linnet said, trying to sound reasonable. "In fact, I don't want to collaborate with you any more than you want to work with me."

He snorted. "You probably came here with that in mind," he said cynically. "You probably see working with me as a way to turn yourself into a respectable writer."

That stung. Linnet stared at him, willing herself not to get angry. She tried to remind herself that he had been hurt by Glenn's suggestion, that he was lashing out because he didn't know what else to do.

"I already am a respectable writer," she said quietly, "and I certainly don't need to work with you to prove it."

"Then why did you talk Grandfather into this harebrained scheme?"

"I didn't talk him into it," she repeated. "He seems to feel that I can add something to your book."

"What could *you* possibly add to my book?"

"The human touch, perhaps," she suggested, trying not to grow angry. "The characters in your books . . ."

"They are not characters," Jon interrupted. His voice was tight. "They are historical figures."

"Historical figures, yes. But at one time they were human beings with the same passions and feelings that people experience today. You don't seem to realize that. Perhaps that's why Glenn wants me to work with you.''

Again Jon snorted. ''That's ridiculous. It's far more likely that you've managed to work your way into Grandfather's affections and he's made this absurd suggestion for your benefit, not for mine.''

Even as he said it, though, Jon knew it wasn't true. Linnet was far too honest a person to use Glenn that way. As he realized the unfairness of his accusation, a little of his anger left him.

For her part, Linnet did her best to ignore Jon's suggestion that she was using Glenn to further her own career.

''Why exactly don't you want to work with me?'' she asked, suddenly taking the offensive. ''I'm just as much a professional as you are.''

''I would hardly call our styles of writing compatible, would you? You said it yourself. Passions and feelings are what concern you, while I try to set my theories down in a clear, concise manner, without sentimentality getting in the way.''

''Sentimentality?'' Linnet asked.

He gestured impatiently. ''Sentimentality,'' he repeated firmly. ''In my books, you won't find emotion warping facts. History isn't about love and hate; it isn't that simple. In fact,'' he went on, ''life isn't as simple as it's made out to be in the kind of books you write.'' There was just the faintest trace of a sneer in his voice.

Linnet was annoyed, but she tried not to show it.

''I think you're overlooking the role love plays in people's lives,'' she told him quietly.

Jon gave her a skeptical look. ''If you'd like to talk about sex . . .''

''I wouldn't like to talk about sex,'' Linnet interrupted coolly.

"Why not? You certainly have enough torrid sex scenes in your books to indicate that you realize it's sex, not love, that motivates people."

"I don't write sex scenes, I write love scenes," Linnet said with quiet dignity.

"Love scenes, sex scenes," he said. "I don't see much difference."

"Don't you?" Linnet asked a little sadly. "I'm sorry to hear that."

Jon looked annoyed. "We're wandering from the point a little, aren't we? I don't want one of my books to deteriorate into a series of love scenes."

"There is nothing wrong with a love scene," Linnet said. Why didn't he go, she was wondering. Surely there was nothing more to discuss.

"Not in its proper place," he said with a sudden gleam in his eye. "Its place isn't in one of my books."

"I'm not suggesting that we include any spicy love scenes in your book," she told him a little wearily. Her voice grew tart. "Though it might increase your sales."

Jon ignored that.

"This is the proper place for a love scene," he said, gesturing around him. "The bedroom."

In three strides he was in front of her. He stared down at her face for one heart-stopping moment before taking her into his arms. Linnet had only a fleeting second to remember what she had thought as he entered her bedroom. She had wondered if he would kiss her.

Before her thoughts could go any farther, his lips were on hers and Linnet felt herself respond. For a moment her mouth was soft and yielding. For a moment her body fit against his. But only for a moment.

"I told Glenn I'd work with you," she said, forcing herself to step out of the circle of his arms. She could hear the frantic beating of her heart and wondered if he could hear it too. "Nothing else." Keeping her voice steady was an effort, but she managed it.

Jon jammed his hands into his pockets and looked down at her.

"You're a cool one, aren't you?" he said.

His voice was as steady as hers, though Linnet didn't think it cost him as much as it did her to keep it that way. "Last night you seemed to enjoy my kisses, but today . . ."

"Since you've refused to work with me," Linnet said, "I don't think we have anything more to discuss."

He laughed harshly. It suddenly seemed to him there was no place for him in her life or in his grandfather's. The two of them had drawn together, leaving him on the outside. He wasn't going to let that happen.

"You're wrong," he said. "I've changed my mind. We are going to work together on Grandfather's biography. In fact, I think I'll tell him about it right now." He turned and left the room abruptly.

Linnet heard his words with a feeling of dismay. How could they work together? What had made him change his mind? She stared after him uncomprehendingly.

How in the world was she going to juggle her obligations so that she could work with Jon? She had been so sure he would refuse to work with her that she hadn't really considered it. Now, though, she'd have to find a way to manage, or Glenn would be hurt.

Chapter Eight

Linnet was disgusted with herself. She was in love—helplessly, hopelessly in love. There was no denying it, she thought glumly. When Jon smiled at her, her spirits soared. When he was nowhere near, she longed for his presence. When he touched her, she melted. No, she couldn't deny those symptoms. She recognized them as surely in herself as she did in her heroines. She had fallen in love with Jon before she had been able to stop herself.

Falling in love was supposed to be a glorious experience but, for Linnet, it had turned out to be nothing short of a disaster. It wasn't falling in love itself that was so bad, she told herself with a heartfelt sigh, it was falling in love with Jon—Jon, who could be so warm and understanding, so kind and gentle; Jon, who could be so cruelly scornful.

For years she had kept herself aloof from men who were interested only in a casual relationship. For years she had experienced love only through the books she wrote as she waited for the man of her dreams. Now that he had come along, something was wrong, drastically wrong. Being in love was making her completely miserable. She couldn't sleep, and work on *A Summer Rhapsody* had come to a virtual standstill.

The days were filled with a kind of hectic routine. Just after sunrise, Linnet went horseback riding, sometimes with Jon, sometimes without him. When Jon was with her, the morning's ride became the high point of her day. She always made it a point to steer the conversation away from their work. They talked of Glenn, the ranch, or anything else that came to mind—anything but their work. During those rides, Linnet found it easy to convince herself that Jon felt something for her. They shared a rapport that she almost believed could bridge any difficulty or difference of opinion they might have. It was a heady feeling.

In the afternoons, though, when Glenn was resting and she and Jon were in his library working, that rapport disappeared. At those times, Jon was cool to the point of almost ignoring her completely. He had placed a very small desk in one corner of the room and there Linnet sat, facing the wall, trying to do her part.

She felt as though she were struggling in the dark. Jon paid no attention to her and, if he read any of the episodes from Glenn's life that she wrote up, he didn't mention it. He seemed intent on keeping her role to a minimum.

The collaboration was, as Linnet had feared, something of a disaster. Time after time, she was tempted to call it quits. Three things stopped her: Glenn's feelings, her love for Jon, and her pride. Though the afternoons were sheer torture, she was determined to see the project through.

"Have you read any of the vignettes of your grandfather's life that I've written up?" Linnet asked after they had been working together for a couple of weeks.

She wanted some kind of feedback from Jon, even if she

had to push him to get it. She had to know what her part in the book was to be. Otherwise, she was merely wasting her time. And, as the deadline for her own book came closer, her time became more valuable.

"Yes, I've read them," Jon said briefly. He bent over the papers on his desk.

She waited a moment, but Jon said no more.

"Well?" she asked. She was determined to make Jon commit himself one way or the other.

He shrugged. "What is it you want me to say?"

"I want you to tell me what you think of them," she said in exasperation. "They're only rough ideas, of course, but I think they show the love your grandmother and grandfather had for each other." Her exasperation turned to eagerness as she talked. "They help to round out the character of your grandfather; they show that love was as important in his life as money and power. We could use them to highlight various stages in his life."

"I don't think so," Jon said deliberately. He held up his hand as he saw her start to speak. "Oh, they're well written; I'm not saying they aren't. No one, least of all me, would deny that you write well."

Linnet was elated. That was the first compliment he had ever paid her work. His next words smothered her joy.

"But, as I've told you before, I'm not going to let you turn my book into one of your love stories. This is a serious biography and I want it to have dignity and stature—not sloppy sentimentality."

Linnet felt as though she had just been doused with a bucket of cold water.

"Do you think there is no dignity in the love Glenn had—and still has—for his wife?" she asked incredulously.

"No, of course I don't think that," he said with elaborate patience. "But I do think it has no place in a book like this."

His condescension infuriated Linnet. She hated being patronized. He was talking to her as if she were a child. What was more, she was beginning to get the idea that he had no intention of letting her do anything on the book at all. He was willing to let her sit there staring at the blank wall and that was about it.

"What exactly do you want me to do?" she asked quietly. "We're supposed to be collaborating, but so far you've rejected every idea I've proposed."

"I don't really know what you can do," he admitted. His eyes passed over her appraisingly. "I suppose you could always do the typing."

The typing! Linnet was so furious she couldn't speak. She hated to type. She typed her own manuscripts, of course, but that was only because she didn't trust them to anyone else. She had no intention of typing for him.

"Do you take dictation?" he asked. He didn't seem to be aware of how angry she was. "Perhaps I could dictate to you."

Jon looked sincerely interested in her answer, so sincerely interested that Linnet was sure he was trying to make her angry. He was succeeding too, though she had no intention of showing him that.

"You don't want a collaborator," she told him, keeping her anger hidden. "You want a secretary."

She had had enough. She wanted no more of this. She couldn't sit there, day after day, eating her heart out. She stood up.

Jon looked startled. "Where are you going?"

"To my room," she answered calmly. "When you find something for me to do, I'll be glad to help. Until then, I'll use the afternoons for my own work."

She really did need to spend more time on her own book, she thought ruefully. The few hours she snatched here and there weren't enough, not with a deadline looming ahead of her. And especially not when thoughts of Jon were playing havoc with her ability to concentrate.

She moved toward the door, congratulating herself on the calm way she had handled the situation. She was completely unprepared for the sudden tears that filled her eyes and threatened to spill down her cheeks. She had to get out of the room before she embarrassed herself. She walked toward the door, keeping her head averted. When she reached the door, however, she furiously blinked back her tears and turned to face him.

"Have you ever read one of my books, Jon?"

When he didn't answer right away, she went on.

"I thought not." A little steel entered her voice. "Don't you think you should put aside your prejudices long enough to learn something about a subject you're so quick to criticize? For someone who prides himself on his ability to analyze facts and weigh evidence before reaching a conclusion, you're awfully closed-minded."

At that point, Linnet didn't really care if she made him angry.

Jon stared at her thoughtfully. He wanted to dismiss her words, but he knew he couldn't. She was just leaving the room when he spoke.

"Wait," he said. "Don't go yet. I think we should talk."

She turned back. "Do you really think that will help?" she asked a little wearily.

Jon crossed the room, took her arm, and led her back to her chair. He leaned against his desk and stared down at her pensively. His arms were folded across his chest.

"You may be right," he said slowly. "Perhaps I have been a little unfair."

Linnet sat forward in her chair. She suddenly remembered the look on Jon's face when he came to her room after

Glenn had suggested the collaboration. She had thought then that he was hurt. Perhaps his grandfather's idea still hurt him.

"Is there anything else that bothers you about working with me?" she asked.

His face grew impassive. "Like what?"

She stood up nervously. She wanted to reach out to him, but she wasn't sure it was wise. "I thought you might be a little put out by the fact that your grandfather asked you to work with someone else," she said, picking her words carefully.

Carefully chosen though they were, her words elicited an angry response from Jon.

"Are you suggesting that I'm hurt because Grandfather doesn't think my work is good enough without some outside help? Or are you suggesting that I'm jealous?"

Linnet quailed at the look on his face, but she held her ground.

"I'm not suggesting either of those things, Jon," she told him earnestly. "I just want to know how you feel. I want you to be honest with me. Then, maybe we can work together after all."

He turned and walked over to the large window looking out on the valley. Linnet stared at his back in dismay. She had made things worse, not better. The silence stretched out until she didn't know how to break it.

"All right," Jon said finally. "Perhaps you're right. Perhaps I am a little jealous, a little hurt."

The bleakness of his voice pierced Linnet. She had to stop herself from rushing to his side and taking him in her arms.

Jon turned away from the window and sank into his desk chair. Everything about him radiated unhappiness.

Compassion swept over Linnet, pushing away thoughts of what might or might not be wise. Before she realized it, she had crossed the room and dropped to her knees by his side. She reached out and took his hand in hers.

"There is no reason for you to feel that way," she told him as she stared into his face. "Your grandfather has nothing but respect and admiration for your work. He has told me so, time after time."

He stared back at her, and the look in his eyes was so raw, so disbelieving, that Linnet could hardly bear it. She hadn't realized just how much she loved Jon until now. His pain had become her own.

"Then why is he so insistent that we work together?" he asked harshly.

Linnet cast about for something that would reassure him.

"I don't think he cares about the book at all," she said at last. "I think he's just using it as an excuse to throw us together. He's playing matchmaker."

It wasn't the wisest thing she could have said, but it seemed to be working. His features relaxed and some of the rigidity left his body.

"He hasn't been very successful at it, has he?" Jon asked, with an unexpected flash of rueful humor.

"No, he hasn't," Linnet agreed. She couldn't very well tell him that Glenn had been spectacularly successful with her.

Jon's eyes were on her face, and Linnet forced herself to meet them calmly. She didn't want him to know of the anguish his pain had caused her. She suddenly became aware of the way she was kneeling beside him and the way her hands held his. Stiffly, she got to her feet. As she moved away from him, she forced herself to harden her heart.

"I think we need a break," he said. His eyes were still on her face. Now, though, they were filled with speculation, not pain. "Let's go for a drive."

Linnet started to refuse. She was exhausted. It had been a very emotional afternoon.

"Please come," Jon said, coaxingly. "I'm going to see whether I can find a copy of one of your books. I think I owe it to myself—and you—to read one."

The look he gave her was so winsome and appealing that Linnet's heart melted. Jon could always do that to her, she reflected as her exhaustion disappeared and her spirits started to climb.

"I'll get my purse," she said.

She hurried up to her room, pausing only long enough to brush her hair.

"Where are we going?" she asked idly as Jon drove his powerful sports car away from the ranch. The top was down, and she leaned back and let the wind rush through her hair.

"I thought we'd drive over to Solvang," Jon answered. "Originally it was a Danish settlement, and now it's something of a tourist attraction."

"I've heard of it," Linnet told him, "but I've never taken the time to pay it a visit."

"There's a good bookstore there and a little French bistro where we can have some wine or coffee."

"That sounds lovely," she said. "You know, I'm beginning to regret never having bothered to come up here before." The green of the rolling hills, highlighted by vivid yellow wild flowers, delighted her.

"To me, this is the most beautiful part of California." Jon reached over and laid his hand on hers. "I'm glad you appreciate it."

"Who wouldn't?" she murmured.

At the touch of his hand on her bare skin, her breath caught and her heart began to race. Why was it Jon could elicit such a reaction? No other man had ever been able to cause anything even close to what she was feeling now.

"You'd be surprised at all the people who don't appreciate this kind of beauty,'' he was saying. "People who prefer the crowds and pollution of the city. The moment I saw you, though, I knew you weren't like that.''

His smile made Linnet feel special, almost cherished.

"Oh, by the way,'' Jon said. "We've been invited to a cocktail party this evening.''

"Why don't you go without me?'' Linnet suggested. She wouldn't know anyone, and she didn't particularly like cocktail parties anyway. "I'm sure no one will care.''

"I'm sure they will,'' he retorted. "Miguel de la Guerra, the owner of that vineyard I told you about, specifically asked me to bring you.'' He gave her hand a squeeze. "Apparently people have heard you're staying at the ranch and they want to meet you. I accepted for both of us. I hope you don't mind.''

Surprisingly enough, Linnet did not mind. She idly watched the scenery go by, more aware of the pressure of his hand on hers than of the green-clad hills. He seemed to have no inclination to break contact between them, and neither did she. She called herself weak-minded, but she left her hand where it was.

Solvang was a charming little town with a well-stocked bookstore, as Jon had promised. Inside the bookstore, Linnet could barely contain her laughter as Jon stiffly asked the clerk for her books.

"We probably don't have any, but they'd be over there if we do.'' The clerk led him over to a display of romances. "Books by Linnet Brooks usually sell out as soon as they come in. She's very popular, you know.''

"So I understand,'' Jon replied dryly.

"You're in luck,'' the clerk exclaimed suddenly. "Here's her latest one.'' She pulled out a copy of *Morning's Promise*. "It must have been hidden away behind some other books.''

She handed the book to Jon, who took it gingerly.

From the look on his face, Linnet told herself, you'd have thought he had just been handed a poisonous snake. She tried not to laugh as she pretended to examine the store's display of cookbooks.

The clerk gave him a curious look.

"Are you buying this for someone else?" she asked as she rang up the sale.

"No," he told her. "I'm buying it for myself."

"Really?" The look she gave him was even more curious. "We don't have many men customers buying romances. Do you mind if I ask you why you're buying it?"

"For penance," Jon told her.

The clerk looked puzzled as she handed him his change. She obviously had no idea what he was talking about.

"I hope you enjoy it," she said a little doubtfully.

Jon thanked her, then walked over to Linnet.

"Satisfied?" he asked, slipping an arm around her shoulders. "I feel like an utter fool."

"That's probably good for you," Linnet told him laughingly.

"At least she put it in a bag," Jon said as they left the store. "Imagine how I'd feel if someone I knew saw me carrying this thing."

He was so obviously teasing her that Linnet did not take offense. Instead she let herself enjoy the banter they were exchanging and the weight of his arm on her shoulders.

Jon steered her down the street, pointing out sights as they walked. There were occasional windmills creaking in the wind and restored houses called *bindings-vaerk*, with storks perched atop the copper roofs. Eventually, they came to the small cafe Jon had mentioned and had iced coffee under a round umbrella that shielded them from the sun.

"I want to thank you for coming up to the ranch," he told

her, picking up her hand and playing with her fingers. "Grandfather has really enjoyed having you, and so have I."

"You don't always act like it." The words slipped out before Linnet had a chance to think of what she was saying.

"I know I don't."

He caressed her hand, then turned it over and traced the lines on her palm.

"Have you noticed how well we get along when we're not discussing your work?"

She had indeed, but she didn't know he had noticed it too.

"Like that night we went for a walk, for instance."

His voice carried so much meaning that Linnet was transported back to Jon's clearing in the woods. For one brief moment, she imagined the warmth of his lips on hers and the strength of his arms when he held her close. As she relived it, she felt a chill slide down her back. It brought her back to reality. She removed her hand from his and wrapped it around her glass of iced coffee.

"That night was a mistake," she said a little breathlessly. She stared down at the ice in her glass.

"You're not embarrassed by what happened between us, are you?" he asked incredulously.

"Of course I'm not," she lied. "But . . ."

Jon's face changed, and he cursed himself for a fool. A few kisses couldn't mean much to her.

"I wouldn't think a woman like you could be embarrassed about a thing like that," he said aloud.

There was a note to his voice that made Linnet look up quickly. He was watching her with eyes that were strangely intent.

"After all, passion is your stock in trade, isn't it?" No, he thought bitterly. To her, those kisses were probably nothing more than a scene that could be replayed in one of her books.

She ignored his words, wishing she could read his expression. The happiness they had been sharing seemed to be disintegrating before her eyes. Jon had withdrawn into himself, and she was feeling miserable.

"Since we're trying to work together," she said slowly, "I don't think we should be involved in any other way. Surely you can see that."

The look she gave him was so appealing that he could not help but be affected. He studied her silently, wondering what lay behind the imploring look in her eyes. One minute she seemed to care about him, the next she was cool and aloof. And now she seemed to be pleading for his help.

I should have made love to her then, he thought suddenly. She wouldn't have stopped me; she wanted me as much as I wanted her.

Then he remembered the trusting way she had gazed up at him, and his eyes grew even more thoughtful. Was it possible that she was as innocent as her heroines? It seemed unlikely, but he had to find out before she drove him crazy.

Jon had never been tormented by a woman like this. He wanted her more than he had ever wanted any other woman. He wanted to caress her, to stroke her, to make her cry out with delight. And yet, when he'd had the chance, he hadn't taken it. Something he didn't understand had held him back.

It won't happen again, he vowed. When the opportunity came again, and he was sure it would despite her words, he would seize it.

At that thought, his face relaxed into a smile. Seeing it, Linnet relaxed too. Perhaps the afternoon could be salvaged after all.

"Then you agree with me?" she asked.

He looked surprised. "About what?"

"About not getting involved with each other?"

"Oh, that," Jon said. "Of course I don't agree with you. Why shouldn't we enjoy each other in every way we can?"

Linnet gazed at him in dismay. "Our working relationship is difficult enough as it is, without complicating it with . . ." she faltered, not wanting to say the words.

He wasn't nearly so reticent.

"An affair? Isn't that a rather old-fashioned idea for someone who writes so convincingly of passion?"

"You don't know whether I write convincingly or not," she pointed out tartly. "You've admitted that you've never read one of my books."

He held the small brown bag aloft. "I'm about to remedy that."

"Anyway, I don't write about passion. I write about love."

Jon eyed her teasingly. "I'm surprised at you. I thought fiction writers were supposed to be a pretty unconventional lot. You're making yourself sound very old-fashioned and straight-laced."

"I am old-fashioned," she said firmly, "and I'm not the least bit interested in an affair." That would be asking to have her heart broken and, fool though she had proved herself to be where Jon was concerned, she wasn't that foolish.

"I'm not going to push you into anything you don't want," Jon said. His eyes went to her mouth in a suggestive manner. "But that night in the woods . . ."

"That night was a mistake. It won't happen again."

"Won't it?" he murmured. His eyes gleamed wickedly. "We'll see about that."

There was a flash of panic across her face. Jon noticed it,

and it intrigued him. In spite of everything, she couldn't be what she seemed.

Linnet pushed back her chair. She couldn't take any more of this kind of conversation.

"Are you ready to go?"

Much to her surprise, Jon burst out laughing.

"You don't need to worry," he told her. "I'm not going to ravish you here and now."

"I'm hardly worried." Linnet told him coolly. Inside, she was anything but cool. Were her fears so obvious? "But it is getting late and I think we should be going."

He got to his feet and held her chair for her. As Linnet stood, he leaned over and lazily kissed her neck. The touch of his lips on her sensitive skin sent shock waves sliding all the way down to her toes. She stepped away.

"Really, Jon," she said in exasperation. "I thought we just agreed . . ."

"I agreed to nothing," he told her cheerfully. He took her arm firmly, giving her no opportunity to pull back. "Now, let's table the discussion. I want to show you an old church that I think will appeal to you."

He led her down the street, talking determinedly of architecture and the Danes who had settled Solvang. Linnet only half listened.

He's impossible, she found herself thinking. She couldn't decide whether to be amused or exasperated.

Impossible or not, she was in love with him.

At the cocktail party, held in Miguel de la Guerra's centuries-old hacienda, Linnet was the center of attraction. She wore a full-skirted dress with a gently shirred bodice that left her shoulders bare. It was a sophisticated, alluring dress, and she had tossed it into her suitcase on a last-minute impulse. Now she was grateful for the impulse. She looked just the way people expected a romance writer to look: glamorous and worldly.

As she talked to the people around her, Linnet was aware of Jon watching her. He couldn't seem to drag his eyes away. After a while she found it difficult to keep her mind on what she was saying.

She forced herself to pay attention to the woman in front of her who was asking something about contracts. The question dragged on and on and Linnet looked up again. Jon had disappeared. The contracts question finally came to an end. While Linnet answered it, she searched the crowd for Jon. She couldn't find him anywhere.

"Having a good time?" he asked behind her. His breath tickled her ear.

She jumped as his hands dropped possessively over her shoulders. The woman with the question about contracts took the hint and silently drifted away.

"Yes, I am," Linnet said a little nervously.

Jon's hands were now lightly running up and down her arms.

"Everyone is very nice."

Jon turned her so that she was facing him. His hands held her shoulders in a way that was perilously close to an embrace. Linnet hoped her feelings weren't showing.

"Are you enjoying yourself?" Her voice faltered at the look in his eyes.

"No," he said. His voice was uncompromising. "I'm not. I don't like sharing you with all these people."

Linnet stared back at him. His eyes seemed to be everywhere: on her mouth, her cheeks, the hollow at the base of her throat. She suddenly began to feel very warm.

"I wish we had never come," he muttered.

Linnet became aware of the curious glances they were receiving. She stepped back, gently removing herself from

Jon's grasp, in time to see Miguel, their host, coming toward them. He looked troubled.

"Is everything all right?" he asked Jon.

"Of course it is," Jon replied curtly.

Linnet turned to speak to someone who had come up to her and lost track of their conversation.

"You'll excuse us, won't you?" Miguel asked. "I want Jon to try one of my new wines."

"Of course," Linnet murmured.

Though she continued talking to the person in front of her, her eyes followed Jon across the room. When he reached the door, he turned and, through the haze of cigarette smoke, their eyes met in a look so intense that Linnet forgot what she was saying. It wasn't until Jon had left the room that she was able to complete her sentence.

After that, the minutes crawled by. Linnet accepted compliments, laughed at jokes, and praised the beauty of the Santa Ynez Mountains with only half a mind. All the while, she was looking for Jon.

Finally, she saw him coming toward her and her heart lifted.

"Excuse us," he said as he broke into the conversation. His voice was courteous but firm.

The man he had interrupted looked annoyed, but Jon ignored him. He pulled Linnet away from the little knot of people surrounding her and led her outside onto the terrace. Five or six people were milling around aimlessly. Jon swore softly under his breath.

"We're going home," he told her abruptly.

"We can't leave yet," Linnet protested. "We've only been here a little while. What will your friend think?"

"I don't care what he thinks. I'm not going back in there and make small talk while the men paw at you."

"Nobody was pawing at me," she said.

"They wanted to," Jon muttered. "I could see it in their eyes. We're going home where we can be alone."

Linnet made no more protests. She didn't want to stay any more than Jon did. After the crowded, smoke-filled room, the idea of being back at the ranch sounded like heaven.

Jon looked down at her. "Do you want to stay?" The question was jerked out of him.

"No," she whispered. "I don't want to stay."

In silence, they made their way back through the noisy room. Linnet left it to Jon to make their excuses to Miguel. She didn't want to be bothered with thinking of a reason why they were leaving so early. She wanted to concentrate on Jon and the way his arm was wrapped so possessively around her shoulders. She wanted to think about the strange, tortured look she had seen in his eyes. What did it mean?

It wasn't until they were in the car that Linnet began to wonder what would happen once they got back to the ranch.

Jon was as disturbed as she was. From the moment they had arrived at Miguel's hacienda, Jon had been infuriated by the looks of admiration Linnet drew from the men. Just keeping his hands to himself had been a struggle—a struggle he had lost more often than not.

He turned to look at Linnet and found she was staring at him through the darkness. His hand found hers and she clung to it.

Jon resisted the urge to pull off the road and make love to her there and then. He wanted her—oh, how he wanted her—but he wanted her to give herself freely. After the things she had said that afternoon, he wasn't sure she was ready to do that. He might be able to sweep her off her feet, but he knew that wasn't the answer. The kind of pleasure he wanted from Linnet was a two-way street. If she were to regret their lovemaking in the morning, then so would he.

At the ranch, Jon carefully helped Linnet out of the car. Once inside, she began fumbling for words. Jon placed a hand on each side of her face and lifted her head. He dropped a light kiss on her forehead. Then he turned and walked away.

Chapter Nine

"I won't have that kind of thing in my book," Jon exclaimed angrily.

He got up, walked over to Linnet's desk, and dropped the piece of paper he was holding. She picked it up and looked at it apprehensively. As she had feared, it was her latest attempt to inject some vitality into Jon's writing.

"I keep telling you this is a dignified book. There is no place in it for a long discussion of their love."

She sighed. Nothing had changed. Their trip to Solvang and last night's cocktail party seemed to have made things worse, not better.

"But your grandfather wants the love he and your grandmother shared discussed in the book. That's why he wanted me to collaborate with you," she pointed out reasonably.

She was holding onto the edges of her temper despite

Jon's words. By now, she knew how difficult working with him could be. Losing her temper was not going to help matters.

"My grandfather is a romantic like you," Jon said shortly. "What neither of you seems to understand is that romance does not necessarily add to a book's character."

"I understand what you're saying," Linnet said earnestly. "But in a case like this . . ."

"In a case like this," Jon said with cold finality, "the book will be written as I want it. I'm not going to let you turn it into a shapeless love story."

He went back to his desk, making it clear that he had no intention of carrying the conversation any further. Linnet sat at her own desk for a few minutes staring at the wall.

Very quietly, so she wouldn't disturb him, she got to her feet and left the room. She couldn't stay there any longer. She was furious with him. And she was hurt. Despite her attempts to ignore the things Jon said, it upset her when he treated her like a second-class writer. The high-handed way he rejected all her ideas did more than hurt. It left her aching for hours.

Jon watched her go, cursing himself for his lack of tact. He had never had this much trouble getting along with anyone else, man or woman, and he suspected that his problems with Linnet were of his own making. He didn't know why that should be so; he only knew that he always seemed to do or say the wrong thing. He scowled at the door as she quietly closed it behind her, then turned and tried to forget her white, strained face in the mass of notes in front of him.

Linnet went straight to the stable and saddled the horse she rode each morning.

"I will not cry over Jonathan West," she told herself as she threw the saddle over the horse's back. She was not one of her heroines, and she had no intention of behaving like one. She was a successful, well-adjusted woman and no man, not even Jon, was going to reduce her to tears.

Once the horse had been saddled, she ambled along slowly, letting the heat of the day drain away some of her emotion. Presently, she came to a small stream and followed it until it led to the small pond that Jon called the swimming hole. She slid off the back of the horse, kicked off her shoes, sat on a rock, and put her feet in the water.

I should pack up and leave. If it weren't for Glenn, I'd do just that, she told herself. Loving Jon was bringing her far more misery than joy. Linnet did not know how much longer she could take the highs and lows of their relationship. She was beginning to feel so drained that work on her own book was becoming increasingly difficult. By the time night came, she was usually too worn out to concentrate and, as a result, her own work was falling farther and farther behind.

If it weren't for Glenn, she thought she'd leave tomorrow.

Or would she?

Linnet didn't want to think about that. She splashed her feet in the water, trying to forget about Jon and the heartache he had brought her. The sparkling water looked so cool and inviting that it seemed to beckon her. She gazed at it yearningly. It was a hot day and she felt sticky.

Should she go in? She looked around her, then dismissed the idea. It reformed itself almost immediately. No one was within miles. She was completely alone. Why not?

Before she could talk herself out of it, Linnet had slipped off her clothes, leaving them in a little pile beside the rock on which she had been sitting. She hesitated before removing her panties and bra; then, with a feeling of abandon, she added them to the small pile at her feet.

The water was clear and cool and felt heavenly. The arching branches of the trees beside the pond provided a green canopy of leaves that sheltered her from the harsh rays of the sun.

As she paddled about in the water, she could feel her depression begin to lift. She rolled over on her back and floated, enjoying the silky sensation of the water on her bare skin. She should have done this days ago, she thought with a sigh of pleasure.

In the library of the ranch house, Jon threw down his pencil in exasperation and got to his feet. He couldn't concentrate. Thoughts of the expression on Linnet's face kept getting between him and the paper. He knew he was in the wrong, and he had to apologize before he could get any work done.

He checked her room, then went out to the stable. As he had suspected, the horse she usually rode was missing. He saddled Snowdrop, his own horse, and went out to look for her. He knew his chances of finding her were slim, but he had to try. The sooner he apologized, the better. Perhaps then he could get back to work.

It wasn't until he heard the soft whinny of her horse that he realized she was swimming in the pond.

"Slow down, boy," he said to Snowdrop, who was prancing eagerly in place.

He pulled the horse up short and watched for a few moments through the trees. Though he was too far away to see clearly, he could catch tantalizing glimpses of Linnet's alabaster skin glistening in the sunlight. It didn't take him long to realize that she was swimming in the nude.

When he did, Jon very nearly nudged the horse forward. He wanted to shed his own clothes and join her in the water. Without consciously thinking about it, he knew how soft and yielding her damp skin would be; he knew how her cool body would feel against his warm one.

Desire spurted through him. He wanted to hold her, to caress her, to let his hands slide down her body. He wanted it so badly that his own body seemed to grow hotter. He took off the hat he always wore when he rode and fanned himself with it.

A growl of frustration escaped his throat. If only their relationship was less complicated, he thought impatiently. If they had a purely physical relationship, nothing would have kept him from her. But their relationship wasn't purely physical and, somewhat to his surprise, Jon realized that he didn't want it to be. He wanted her body, of course. He wanted it with a hunger he had never experienced before. He also wanted something more. He just didn't know quite what.

Quietly, Jon dismounted and tied his horse to a tree. He knew Linnet would be furious if she even suspected that he was watching her, but he couldn't help himself. Slowly and carefully, he crept through the bushes until he was almost directly across from the spot where she had left her clothes. Jon watched hungrily as Linnet floated lazily on her back. Every now and then she moved her arms and the water washed up over her stomach and breasts. The sun sparkled as it touched her body. Jon felt an almost intolerable pressure growing inside him. He knew he should be ashamed of himself for spying on her this way, but he felt no shame.

Finally, Linnet flipped over, swam a few strokes, then waded out of the water. Jon noted the wet, dark hair that hung down her back and the long, slender legs that carried her to the spot where she had left her clothes.

When she reached that spot, she turned and looked back across the water. For a moment, Jon thought she had seen him. Then, in a languid movement, she raised her arms and with both hands squeezed the water from her hair.

Jon couldn't tear his eyes away. He crouched in the bushes unable to move, barely breathing, as Linnet's body imprinted itself on his senses. Her breasts were full and firm; next to the swell of her hips, her waist curved invitingly.

His eyes, the only part of him that moved, touched all the parts of her body. She had picked up her blouse and was using it to dry herself.

Jon felt sweat break out as she used her blouse to blot the water first from her arms, then her breasts and stomach. Carefully she sat down on the rock and gracefully raised one leg at a time as she dried them.

Again she lifted her arms, this time using her blouse to remove some of the water from her hair.

Jon's mouth was dry, and he licked his lips impatiently as he watched the movement of her body.

Finally, Linnet stood up again. She glanced doubtfully at her underwear, then stepped into her jeans. Slowly, she inched them up her legs and over her hips.

Somewhere inside him, Jon moaned. Almost as though she had heard it, Linnet looked up and glanced around her. Then she shook her head and spread her blouse out on the rock to dry. She sat down again, this time leaning back on her elbows and arching her back as she raised her face to the sun.

Jon could stand it no longer. Every nerve in his body cried out for her. With what little willpower he still retained, he forced himself to crawl back through the bushes and mount his horse. Without realizing where he was going, he rode back toward the house. His mind was filled with what he had just seen, and his body ached with longing. When he came to a small clearing where he could tie up his horse, he stopped. There he flung himself on the ground to wait for Linnet while he cooled down.

Linnet rode back to the house reluctantly. The swim had lifted her spirits temporarily, but she still had to sit across from Jon at dinner. Again she thought of leaving the ranch.

She knew that wouldn't stop her from loving Jon, but it would put an end to the torture of facing him every day.

Ahead of her, she saw Snowdrop tied up beside the path she was on. Her heart sank. If Snowdrop was there, so was Jon. Linnet didn't feel up to talking to him, not yet. She would have ridden on by him with just a nod of acknowledgement if his voice hadn't stopped her.

"Linnet!" he said hoarsely. His voice was low, and there seemed to be a note of pleading in it.

She was so astonished that she stopped her horse.

"I've been waiting for you." He got up, walked over to her, and began toying with her stirrup.

"Waiting for me?" she echoed. "You mean you knew where I was?"

Her heart fluttered wildly. Why, oh why, had she given in to that notion to go swimming? How much had he seen?

"Yes," he said simply. "You seemed to be having a good time," he added with a smile that told her more than she wanted to know.

So he had been close enough to see that she had been swimming in the nude. Linnet didn't look at him. She would have urged her horse forward if he hadn't put his hand in the bridle.

"I want to talk to you."

"What about?" Talking didn't seem to get them anywhere. "If it's about the book, I'm sure it can wait until tomorrow."

"It is about the book and it can't wait." He took the reins from her hands and led the horse a few feet, where he tied it to a tree.

"Get down," he commanded. "I can't apologize while you're sitting up there."

"Apologize?" Linnet was incredulous. She looked at him closely. What was he up to now?

"Apologize," he repeated firmly. "I know when I've been wrong. It doesn't happen often," he added with a smile. "But when it does, I try to rectify the situation."

Linnet looked down at him wonderingly. He was always so composed, so sure of himself. Even at a time like this, he seemed confident and in complete control of the situation. Doesn't he ever have doubts? she asked herself. It certainly didn't seem as though he did.

He reached up and helped her off the horse. Linnet felt the strength of his arms, then the firm planes of his chest and thighs as she slid down the length of his body. Once her feet were on the ground, she stepped quickly away from him. As it was, her body felt warmed by that brief contact.

He let her go, though he refused to relinquish her hand. Holding it tightly, he led her to a section of soft, springy grass, then pulled her down beside him.

Linnet held herself stiffly apart from him. She was beginning to regret getting off the horse. It put her at a disadvantage.

She sat looking at him until she began to see the humor of the situation. Was he really going to apologize? He didn't seem too anxious to begin.

"Well?" she said, prompting him. A ghost of a smile hovered around her lips.

Jon noted the look on her face and gave her a sheepish smile in return. The charm and vulnerability of that smile went a long way toward melting her heart.

"I got you down from your horse to apologize, so I suppose I should." His voice changed. It became more intent. "I'm sorry for the way I've been treating you. The simple fact is that I'm the very devil to be around when I'm starting a new book. Rachel and Hank will testify to that."

Linnet was disappointed. Though he was apologizing as he said he would, she had been hoping for something considerably more personal. She tried to pull her hand loose, but that merely reminded Jon that he was holding it. He began massaging it in an absent-minded sort of way.

Starting a new book is always difficult,'' Jon added. ''But, then, you know that.''

He turned his head to look at her, but she refused to meet his eyes. Instead, she stared down at the ground. It sounded to her as though he was blaming all their difficulties on the fact that he was starting a new book. He didn't seem to realize that their difficulties were a direct result of his attitude toward the kind of writing she did. He refused to take her seriously.

''I've been particularly rough on you,'' he went on, ''because I don't have the focus of the book fully in mind yet. Because of that, I don't know exactly how your ideas will fit in.''

''I've gotten the feeling that they won't fit in at all,'' she told him.

He was still rubbing her hand. The slow, sensuous motion was beginning to have an effect on her, though Jon didn't even seem to be aware of what he was doing.

''May I have my hand back, please?'' she asked. The politeness in her voice didn't quite conceal her irritation.

He looked down at her hand with such surprise that Linnet wondered if he knew he had been holding it.

''Am I rubbing the skin off?'' he asked with a grin. He stopped the massage but still didn't relinquish her hand. I'm sure your work will fit in somewhere,'' he went on more thoughtfully, ''I'm just not sure how. Be patient with me.''

Linnet shook her head, trying to think clearly. It was never easy when Jon was so close. The warmth of his body disrupted her thought processes.

''I don't think it's just a matter of being patient,'' she said slowly, wishing with all her heart that things were that simple. "I'm beginning to think it was a mistake for us to undertake this collaboration."

His eyes narrowed and he looked at her intently. Not for the first time, she wished she knew what he was thinking.

"Why?"

"Isn't it obvious?"

She pushed back a lock of hair from her face. It was starting to dry and had fallen forward. All at once, she wanted a comb. Here she was, sitting next to Jon, with her hair a mess and her clothes still damp. Why couldn't he have waited for a better time to have this little talk? she thought with irritation. Why did he always choose a time when she was at a disadvantage?

"You have no respect for my work," she said, doggedly forcing her thoughts back to the subject they were discussing. "You think reading or writing romance is a waste of time. You've said so time and time again. Given those circumstances, I don't see how we can work together."

"You could change the kind of writing you do," he pointed out. "I could help you."

That made her angry. She snatched her hand from his.

"I have no desire to change the kind of writing I do," she said coldly. "I enjoy what I do. I enjoy writing for people who want to read about love. Love . . ." She paused, searching for the right words. How could she convince a skeptic like Jon of the importance of love?

"I know," he said acidly. "Love makes the world go 'round."

With an effort, Linnet curbed the impulse to lash out at him. That wouldn't do any good. If only she could make him understand.

"Haven't you ever been in love, Jon?" she asked.

"No," he said flatly. "Have you?" His eyes were suddenly watchful.

That was a question she had no intention of answering, not considering the current state of her emotions. Though she ignored it, his question shook her.

"People enjoy reading about love," she told him, as though his question had never been asked. "They enjoy reliving their own experiences or dreaming of a love to come. I admit that my books don't appeal to the intellectual elite or the avant-garde," she went on quietly, "and I don't really care. Do you remember the nurse in intensive care we talked to one night?"

Jon nodded—a little unwillingly, Linnet thought. She couldn't really blame him for not wanting to remember that encounter, she thought with a sudden flash of humor.

"I write for people like her. People who need to escape now and then. Not everyone lives on a ranch in the mountains," she pointed out. "Most people have to cope with things like traffic problems and inflation. They enjoy escapist reading and occasionally even need it. I write for them and I'm glad I can touch their lives, even if it is only for a few hours."

He nodded reluctantly. "I think I can understand that," he admitted slowly.

At his words, Linnet's heart jumped. If she could make him understand, there might be hope for them. She wrapped her arms around her knees and hugged them tightly while she waited for him to go on. Her heart was beating crazily. Could she get through to him?

"As a matter of fact, I've started reading your book—the one I bought in Solvang."

Linnet nodded and hugged her knees more tightly.

"I haven't gotten too far, but already I can see that I have been a little closed-minded."

Linnet had the feeling he was forcing himself to speak. Certainly this couldn't be easy for him.

"Your book isn't at all what I thought it would be," he admitted. "So far, I haven't run into a single bedroom scene." He gave her a slightly crooked grin. "In fact, you seem to deal more with the complexities of human relationships than sex."

"That's what I try to do," she told him, "though, of course, there has to be some sex. My editor . . ."

"Editors are ghouls," Jon put in.

"Not mine," Linnet said.

She pitied any editor who had to work with Jon. His ideas of what a book should be were so rigid and unbending that he probably went through editors like cans of soda pop.

"How many editors have you had?" she asked curiously. His answer didn't surprise her.

"Dozens," he said briefly. He went back to the subject of her writing. "From your book, I'm getting the idea that you think sex and love go hand in hand."

"Yes, I do."

"Then you'd never let your heroines indulge in a little casual sex."

"No, I wouldn't. Sex without love has no meaning. It's merely physical exercise."

He grinned at that. "Perhaps. But it's very pleasant exercise."

Linnet hoped she didn't look as uncomfortable as she felt. She didn't want to discuss anything as intimate as sex with Jon—especially not when he was sitting so close that she could actually feel the heat of his body.

"Does that mean that you . . . ?" He looked at her and his voice trailed off.

Linnet sat terrified. It sounded as though he was going to ask her about her own sex life. What would she say?

She stole a look at him. He was frowning at the ground and, for the first time, Linnet saw that he was unsure of himself. Before she had time to decide what that meant, he went back to what they had been discussing a few moments earlier.

"It's going to take me a while to overcome my prejudices. That's why I'm asking you to be patient. Do you think you can wait?"

"I don't know. I suppose I can try," she said. This is a step in the right direction, she told herself. Perhaps in time . . .

"Good." He slid an arm around her shoulders and pulled her closer. "I know the past few weeks haven't been easy on you. If it's any consolation, they haven't been easy on me either."

"No, I don't suppose they have."

She leaned against him contentedly. The depression she had felt when she set out on her ride was completely gone. It had been replaced by hope, hope that things would somehow work out between them. She rested against him with a feeling of homecoming. Her heart told her this was where she belonged, with Jon, in his arms.

As Jon felt her relax, his arms closed around her and he held her close.

"You're still a little damp," he said teasingly. "Did you enjoy your swim?"

"It was heavenly."

"When I saw you there, I wanted to join you." He broke off as he felt her stir in his arms.

"I'm glad you didn't," Linnet said fervently. Just the thought of it made her knees weak.

"It was a struggle," Jon said with a chuckle. "I could see your beautiful white skin through the trees, and it was all I could do to keep from flinging off my clothes and diving into the water myself."

Linnet shivered. She almost wished he had done just that.

Jon felt the convulsive movement of her body and misinterpreted it.

"Would it have been so terrible if I had gone swimming with you?" he asked.

She didn't want to answer that question. "I think we should be getting back to the house," she said instead. The conversation was getting too personal to suit her. "Glenn will be wondering where we are."

"We have a few moments yet," Jon told her. He held her tightly so that she couldn't get up. "Answer my question."

"Under different circumstances," she said stiffly, "it would have been all right."

He laughed out loud. "What you mean is that it would have been all right if we had been wearing swim suits. But skinny-dipping is out."

"It is definitely out," Linnet said.

Jon tilted her head back and searched her eyes with his. What he saw puzzled him.

"Why?" he asked bluntly.

"Because . . ." Her voice died off. She was in over her head. How could she explain to Jon that she wasn't the kind of person who played at sex? In that respect, she was like her heroines.

"Is it that you don't think of me that way?"

His voice had changed, but Linnet was so caught up in her own feelings that she didn't notice the sudden stiffness of his words.

"Yes," she said gratefully, clutching at the straw he had just offered her. Why hadn't she thought of saying something like that herself?

Because it was so far from the truth, came the answer.

"I don't believe that for a moment," Jon said briefly. "I'll show you why."

He kissed her slowly and deliberately. He kissed her with such force that Linnet didn't even think of resisting.

Instead, she put her arms around his neck and clung to him, returning his kiss passionately.

"Are you sure you don't feel that way about me?" he asked, when their lips parted.

"Well, maybe a little," she answered breathlessly. Her lips felt warm and slightly swollen.

"Good," he said, "because that's how I feel about you."

Again he kissed her, a kiss both teasing and provoking.

"Every time I see you, I want to take you in my arms and kiss you. And I want you to kiss me back." He leaned down and nibbled at her lips. "When we're working together in the library, I have to force myself to concentrate on what's in front of me. I'd much rather be touching and kissing you."

His words left her speechless. She knew exactly how he felt. There had been so many times when she longed to be in his arms. Could it be that Jon was beginning to fall in love with her? A week ago, she would have said that was impossible. But a week ago, she would have said he'd never admit that romance had any merits whatsoever. And today, he had come close to admitting that very thing.

Hope began to grow inside her, and she gave him a tremulous kiss on the strength of it.

"To think you said you weren't interested in an affair," he said teasingly.

At his words, her blood ran cold. She felt as though he had hit her. She should have known, she told herself tiredly. She had been thinking of love and permanence while he was thinking of sex and an affair.

Unsteadily, she got to her feet. Jon didn't try to stop her this time and, at the back of her mind, Linnet was surprised by that. What she didn't realize was that her face had gone white and that Jon was staring at her with considerable confusion.

"I'm *not* interested in an affair," she told him in a voice that was unnaturally calm. She felt numb all over. All her hopes had come crashing down around her.

"Then why did you let me kiss you?" he asked perplexedly.

"I was wrong to kiss you," she said, without really answering his question. "It won't happen again."

"You've said that before," he pointed out. His voice still sounded perplexed.

Linnet winced. She had said it before, several times, in fact.

"This time I mean it." She was struggling for composure. His words had left her shaken.

"We'll see about that."

Jon stood in front of her, his arms at his sides. He made no move to touch her, though he might have if he had known what she was thinking. Linnet ached to be in his arms. Pushing him away and getting to her feet had been one of the hardest things she had ever done. With his arms around her, she had felt at home; she had felt as though she finally belonged somewhere.

"You're not very easy to understand," Jon said as he looked down at her white face.

"Neither are you," she replied with as much spirit as she could muster.

"I don't agree. In this I'm very easy to understand. I want to make love to you. I want to give you pleasure, to . . ."

Linnet could bear no more. She walked around him, being careful not to get too close, and untied her horse. Before Jon could help her, she was in the saddle and riding back to the house.

Jon stared after her blankly. What had he said that had sent her off like that? She had enjoyed his kisses, he told himself. He was sure of that, no matter what she said. He should have seized the opportunity and pressed his advantage.

He was almost sure she wouldn't have resisted. But something had held him back; something new in his feelings for her. It had kept him from making her his.

With sudden anger, he too headed back to the house.

Chapter Ten

Two A.M.! Linnet thought in disgust. She glared at the clock almost as though it was the clock's fault she couldn't sleep when in reality it was Jon who was to blame, if anyone was.

That wasn't fair either, she thought, sitting up and staring ahead of her in the dark. Through the window she could see part of the valley illuminated by twinkling starlight. Jon couldn't help it that she had fallen in love with him any more than she could help the fact that he wanted to have an affair with her.

"I feel like one of my own heroines," she grumbled out loud as she threw back the sheet and slipped out of bed.

She knew one thing. She wasn't going to lie there and worry for another hour or so before sleep finally claimed her. She was going for a walk. Jon had made it obvious that he enjoyed her, but he had made it equally obvious that he didn't love or respect her. Worrying about it wasn't going to change things.

Even at their worst, her heroines had never been as weak-minded as she was, she told herself disgustedly as she stole quietly down the stairs.

The house seemed quiet, for which Linnet was grateful. She had no desire to run into Jon. In the dark, she made her way across the hall and out the front door.

Of course, she thought as she hurried away from the house, in some of her books an unexpected, late-night meeting under the moon and stars was inevitable. For a moment she was almost sorry life wasn't like her books. Then she forced herself to be practical. A night of kisses would all too quickly turn into a morning of regrets.

Upstairs, in his bedroom, Jon was staring pensively out of the window. He had just finished *Morning's Promise*, Linnet's latest book, and he was impressed in spite of himself. He couldn't deny that the book was well thought out and well written.

The love scenes in particular, he thought, were powerfully and realistically done. The thought disconcerted him, particularly after the way she had acted that afternoon. He stared out into the night, wondering about the love scenes, until he saw Linnet slip outside. At the sight of her clad only in a short gown and robe, he was lashed by an unexpected jealousy that he didn't stop to analyze. Instead, he left his room and went downstairs to confront her.

He found her standing under a tree, staring out over the moonlit valley. She jumped and spun around as she heard him approach.

"You startled me!" Her words came out jerkily, and she knew the sudden pounding of her heart was not the result of fear alone.

"I'm sorry. I didn't mean to frighten you."

His eyes moved slowly down her scantily clad body. The moon provided just enough light for him to see the curves of her body beneath the tightly sashed robe.

Linnet's hand went to her throat. Her breath caught, and she stepped back into a shadow where he couldn't see her as clearly. His eyes had made her uncomfortably aware of the fact that she wore nothing beneath her short, thin nightdress. Though her robe offered some protection from his gaze, it wasn't much. Her heart was beating so loudly that she wondered if he could hear it.

Life does imitate fiction after all, she thought. This could be a scene straight from one of her books. Though she had wished for such a thing earlier, now she wasn't quite so sure she wanted to face him. She knew it wasn't wise. Nothing could come of this but more heartache. Dreaming of his kisses under the moonlight was one thing; actually experiencing them was another.

Through the darkness, Linnet could see the desire in Jon's eyes. He was staring at her hungrily.

"I couldn't sleep," she said breathlessly. "I came outside hoping a walk would help me relax."

He didn't answer. She began to feel a little frightened. He continued to stare at her almost greedily. The shadows didn't seem to be offering much protection after all.

"Couldn't you sleep either?" she asked.

Though she could hardly speak, she felt she had to say something. The look in his eyes made her want to turn and run, though she had the feeling he wouldn't let her run far. He was clearly angry about something, yet he also looked as though he wanted to devour her. She peered past him into the darkness, fervently wishing she had never left the house.

"Couldn't you sleep either?" she asked again. She had to break through whatever it was that was holding him spellbound.

"I just finished your book," he said in a voice that was low and husky.

"What did you think of it?" she asked cautiously. She

shivered slightly. The night air was beginning to feel cool. This was hardly the place for such a conversation, but she thought it might be better to keep him talking. He looked tense, and it was obvious he was holding some emotion in check. His eyes held secrets she couldn't begin to understand.

"I thought it was very well written."

Linnet had the feeling he wasn't paying much attention to their conversation. His eyes were now moving down her body again, more slowly this time, and he took a step toward her.

Instinctively, she took a step backward and found herself up against the trunk of the tree.

"Does that mean you liked it?"

He smiled; she thought his smile was mocking.

"Let's just say I was impressed. You write with such force and believability that I almost have the feeling you've experienced all the emotions you write about."

"I've hardly done that," Linnet said. "That would be impossible, wouldn't it?"

"Would it?" he asked idly.

He lifted his eyes to hers and held them in a gaze she could not break. She stood with her back to the tree, wanting to run, wanting to tear her eyes from his. But she couldn't. Even though he wasn't touching her, Jon was holding her there.

"Of course it would," she said, trying to keep her mind on the conversation.

She was no longer shivering from the coolness of the air. Her trembling was caused by the look on his face.

"You know yourself that a writer has to rely on imagination and instinct."

"You certainly do it well. So well, in fact, that I could swear . . ." He broke off and took another step. It brought him only inches away from her.

They were so close that Linnet could feel his warmth. She would have taken a step away from him if there had been any place to go and if his eyes were not pinning her to the tree.

"I've underestimated you," he went on. His voice had become a lazy drawl. "Underestimated you badly."

He raised his hand and gently touched her cheek with his finger. Slowly he traced a course down her cheek, around her trembling lips, and down the line of her throat.

Linnet's skin began to tingle, and she fought the urge to run. She was sure any movement she made would put her in Jon's arms. He'd see to that.

"Are you ready to admit that romance writers aren't so terrible after all?" she said teasingly, trying desperately to inject a little humor into a situation that was threatening to overwhelm her with its intensity.

"Not this romance writer, anyway," he said.

His finger was still moving down her neck. Near the base of her throat, he encountered her pulse. It was fluttering wildly.

"I can feel your heart beating here," he said, "and here."

His hand slid farther down until it rested on her breast.

Linnet felt her knees give way, and she was grateful for the support of the tree. His touch scorched her, and her heart began to beat even more erratically, if that were possible.

"You aren't afraid, are you?" he asked. It sounded as though he, too, was beginning to have trouble breathing.

Not of you, Linnet thought, only of myself. How easily his touch could convince her to betray herself. She took his hand in one of her own and lifted it from her breast.

"You know how I feel about this," she said as steadily as she could.

"I know how you say you feel," he answered.

His free hand, the one she wasn't holding, slid under Linnet's hair and around the back of her neck, leaving tiny chills behind it.

"And I know what the beating of your heart tells me. It tells me that you want me as much as I want you."

"No," Linnet said.

She made her voice icy, hoping it would throw a little cold water on his desire—and on her own. She tried to step away from him.

"I think I should go in now."

"Before it's too late for you to go? Isn't that what you really mean?"

"No, that's not what I mean. Jon . . ." Panic was beginning to fray the edges of what little composure she retained.

"Surely you aren't ready for bed," he said, interrupting her. "At least not alone. The way your heart is beating, I don't think you could sleep. Not yet, anyway. Perhaps later."

He was so close now that she could feel his breath on her face. His lips brushed hers slowly and lightly, but not so lightly that Linnet didn't feel the caress in every part of her. Even as the shock waves of his kiss were sliding down her spine, she knew she had to put a stop to this. Now, while she still wanted to.

"No, Jon," she said again, but her voice had lost its conviction.

"Yes, Linnet," he whispered. His lips brushed hers for a second time. This kiss was as tantalizingly slow as the first one, but it was more intense. With a sigh, she swayed toward him. His arms went around her and he pulled her against him eagerly.

"You see?" His voice was hoarse. "You do want me. I've wanted you since the first moment I saw you, and now I'm going to have you."

Linnet barely heard his words. For the first time, she was experiencing the feelings and sensations she had written about for years. For the first time, she was finding out what the physical side of love really meant.

Jon's mouth was warm and urgent against hers. Linnet wrapped her arms around his neck, running her fingers up through his thick, silver hair. He bent her body backward, pressing her against him as he did so. There was a feeling of rightness in being in his arms and she gloried in it.

His kisses grew deeper and more intense and Linnet responded with a blind instinct that would have astounded her if she had been thinking clearly.

Before she quite realized it, Jon had lowered her onto the soft, springy ground. The fresh scent of newly grown grass mingled with Jon's clean scent as he lay down beside her. He fumbled with the sash on her robe and when he had untied it, he leaned on one elbow and stared down at her. His other hand rested on her stomach.

Linnet opened her eyes and looked wonderingly up at him. Gently she caressed his cheek, then her fingers slid down to his chest. Beneath her hand, she could feel the thundering of his heart.

"I've waited so long for this," he murmured. "You'll never know how many times I've had to stop myself from taking you in my arms and caressing you."

He began nibbling at her neck and his lips sent hot chills down her back.

"How many men have made love to you like this?" he mumbled against her neck. His voice sounded tortured.

Linnet paid no attention to his words. It was all she could do to handle the onslaught of new emotions she was experiencing. His lips returned to hers, his tongue probing urgently. His obvious passion enflamed her own desire.

"You're so beautiful, Linnet." He began kissing her cheeks, her forehead, her neck. "I can't resist you."

Linnet let her head drop back to give his mouth more freedom. The sensations he was producing were exquisite.

"How many men like me have you captivated, then used as fodder for your books?" he asked hoarsely.

Those words sunk in. Linnet froze. Surely he couldn't think that of her! Confusedly her mind went over the last few minutes and dredged up something else he had said. How many men have made love to you? he had asked. She had been so caught up in passion that she had paid no attention.

Now, though, she pushed him away and sat up in horror. Her heart felt as though it had broken. She scrambled to her feet. Jon reached up for her and would have pulled her back down to him had she not stepped away.

"What is it? What's wrong?" He got to his feet and peered at her through the darkness.

Linnet stared back at him and, in the moonlight, he could see that her eyes were wide with shock.

"Surely you don't think that of me," she whispered.

"Think what?" He sounded impatient as he reached for her again.

Linnet kept out of his way without even realizing it. All she could think of was the dreadful accusation he had made.

"That I use men for material for my books." It sounded so horrible when she said it that she wanted to cover her ears. "You can't believe that." Her eyes were imploring. "Not after . . ."

"Not after the way you kissed me?" He laughed and his laughter had a harsh ring to it. "If anything, that merely confirms my theory."

She stared back at him disbelievingly. "Couldn't you tell . . . ?" she began brokenly. Her voice trailed off. She couldn't continue.

"Couldn't I tell what?" he asked sharply. His eyes studied her face intently.

"Nothing," she said tiredly.

Her pride wouldn't allow her to state the obvious—that no man had ever stirred her the way Jon had, that no man had ever been allowed close enough to stir those feelings. If he couldn't see it for himself, she wasn't going to point it out to him. Not after the things he had said, not after the accusation he had made. She had some pride left. Enough, anyway, to keep her from making a complete fool of herself.

She turned away and started back toward the house. She had to get away from him before she broke down completely. Already she could feel tears threatening to spill over, tears she had vowed she would not shed over Jon.

"Wait!" he called as she hurried away from him. "Linnet!"

She didn't answer. She didn't even pause. A moment later, she was swallowed up by the dark.

Jon watched her go in confusion. There was a deep ache inside him that he couldn't quite identify. The sight of her shocked face filled his mind. Could he have been wrong? Had he jumped to the wrong conclusion? He stared into the darkness where she had disappeared. Surely not, he told himself. She couldn't be the innocent she seemed. In this day and age, it was impossible. And yet . . .

He, too, started back toward the house.

You look ghastly, Linnet told her reflection. She was staring into the mirror, brushing a little color onto her pale face. She couldn't do much for the dark circles under her eyes though. They were a direct result of her sleepless night, and there was no makeup that would hide them. She brushed her hair irritably, then reluctantly went downstairs to breakfast. With any luck, she thought, Jon would not be there.

She wouldn't have gone down herself if it hadn't been for Glenn. He had been having breakfast with them for the past week or so, and she didn't want him to worry about her absence. Besides, there was something she had to tell him.

She was in luck. Though there was a place laid for Jon, he was not there. She bent to kiss Glenn, then sat down in her own chair wondering how best to tell him of the decision she had come to early that morning. She gazed out over the valley, hoping for inspiration. She was going to miss that view. Over the last few weeks, it had become a part of her. Nevertheless, she had to get away—today.

"You look tired," Glenn said at once. He scrutinized her face. "Have you been overdoing it?"

"I am tired," she confessed. "It's Brad and Joanna. They've been causing me a lot of problems again."

This was partially true. Though Brad and Joanna hadn't kept her up last night, they had kept her awake countless other nights.

"Oh yes, Brad and Joanna. It's been so long since you mentioned them that I'd almost forgotten they existed, so to speak," he said. "What are they up to now?"

"Nothing, absolutely nothing," she told him. "I'm coming to the end of the book now, and I can't seem to get them together. Every time I think things are going to work out for them, one of them does something to put a spoke in the wheel. They seem to have minds of their own," she added ruefully, "and they don't want to do what I want them to do."

"I'm sure that's very annoying," Glenn said sympathetically. He studied her face shrewdly. "Is anything else bothering you?"

All at once, Linnet saw her opportunity. She took it.

"Well, yes, there is something else," she said, crossing her fingers against the lie she was going to tell. "I was talking to my editor last night, and she wants me to fly east for a few days."

It wasn't true, of course, but she had to get away from Jon, and a sudden trip to New York was the only way she could think of doing it without hurting Glenn. That she couldn't bear to do, even now, when Jon's words had shattered her heart into a thousand pieces. The old man meant too much to her.

His face fell. "Is that really necessary?"

She could tell that the prospect made him unhappy. "I'm afraid it is," she said gently. "There are some people I have to see and some problems that have to be sorted out."

That, at least, was the truth. Jon was a big problem, the biggest of her life, and she had to decide what to do about him.

"Then I suppose you'll have to go," he said regretfully. "But you'll be back soon, won't you?"

"As soon as I can," she promised. "I shouldn't be gone any more than a week." That was a rash promise, considering her feelings. She never wanted to return, not if it meant seeing Jon again.

"A week is a long time at my age," Glenn told her. "When you're old, you feel that each day is a gift—and I want to share each day with you."

Linnet was so touched that she had to blink back sudden tears. For a moment she almost hated Jon for putting her in this position.

"When do you have to leave?" Glenn asked.

"My plane leaves this afternoon. I'll just have time to stop at my house and pick up some clothes."

Glenn's eyes were thoughtful as they studied her face. "That's very sudden, isn't it? Is there anything else that's upsetting you? Jon, for instance?"

"No, of course not," she said, lying again. How could

she tell this dear old man that his grandson was making her miserable?

"You know I'll miss you," Glenn told her. "You will hurry back, won't you?"

"Hurry back from where?" asked a voice in the doorway behind them.

It was Jon. Linnet stiffened. She let Glenn answer.

"Linnet has to go to New York for a few days. I'm trying to get her to promise not to stay away too long."

"This is rather sudden, isn't it?" Jon asked. He gave her a searching look.

She nodded wordlessly, again letting Glenn speak for her.

"It's her editor," he explained. "She wants Linnet in New York as soon as possible."

"Does she?" Jon's eyebrows rose fractionally. "When are you leaving?"

Linnet finally found her voice. "This afternoon. I was telling Glenn that I'll have just enough time to stop by my house and pick up some clothes."

She lifted her eyes and met his gaze steadily. She was determined not to let him see how he had hurt her.

His eyebrows rose even higher, but Linnet did not let it disconcert her. Let him think whatever he wants, she told herself.

"I missed you this morning when I went riding," he said, much to her surprise.

Linnet tried not to let her astonishment show. Surely he hadn't expected her to turn up that morning as though nothing had happened? Was he that sure of her? Her astonishment turned to anger.

"I had so many things to do," she said vaguely. "Plane reservations, hotel reservations, that kind of thing."

If it weren't for Glenn, she was thinking, she'd tell him

exactly what she thought of him. She'd let him know how low she thought he was. After last night . . .

She pushed back her chair and got to her feet. She couldn't eat another bite of breakfast, not with Jon sitting so calmly across the table from her. All she had to do was look at him and she heard again the cruel things he had said.

"I've got a little bit of packing yet to do," she said to Glenn. "I'll see you before I go."

Jon had also gotten to his feet. "I'll walk you to your room. There are some things I think we should discuss."

Linnet started to object but stopped herself. Anything she said would arouse Glenn's curiosity. They left the deck in a silence Linnet had no intention of breaking. She had nothing to say to Jon.

It wasn't until they were climbing the stairs that Jon spoke.

"Running away?" he asked.

Linnet gave him a quick glance. She had expected to find a mocking look on his face, but instead he seemed troubled.

"From what?" she asked lightly. "I've got to go to New York on business. That's all there is to it."

They were walking down the hall now. In a few more steps, they would be at her door.

"About last night—" he began.

Linnet winced. She wanted to forget last night had ever happened. She had practically offered Jon her heart and, in return, he had accused her of using him to get material for her books.

No, last night was one thing she definitely did not want to discuss.

At last they were at her door. The walk down the hall had seemed endless to Linnet. She grasped the doorknob gratefully. Just as she pushed open the door, Jon covered her hand with his.

"I think we should talk," he said firmly, giving her a determined look.

She slipped into her room, then turned to face him.

"And I don't think we have anything to talk about," she replied evenly.

With a quiet finality, she closed the door in his face.

Chapter Eleven

New York was in the midst of a heat wave. There was not a breath of fresh air anywhere. Normally Linnet enjoyed the city. She liked its vitality and its restless energy. Now, though, she found the city noises irritating and the tall buildings that blocked out the sun suffocating.

She had traveled three thousand miles to get away from Jon, and instead she found that he was in her thoughts more than ever. Hot, humid New York made her homesick for the crisp, clean air of the ranch and, any way she looked at it, the ranch meant Jon.

Six days later, sick at heart, she boarded a flight back to Santa Barbara. The trip to New York hadn't enabled her to conquer her love for Jon as she had hoped, but it had taught her that she couldn't continue to work with him. And she couldn't go on living in his house, no matter how much she yearned to be back at the ranch, no matter how much Glenn pleaded with her to stay.

Linnet rubbed her tired eyes as the plane lifted off. Six

days in New York hadn't even left her well rested. She had
lain awake night after night, tossing and turning, yearning
for something she and Jon could never have. Now she was
near the end of her emotional tether. She wanted to get
home and try to rebuild her life. But before she could do
that, she had to tell Glenn she would not be coming back to
the ranch. She wasn't looking forward to that, but it had to
be done.

Once she was back in Santa Barbara she didn't waste any
time. She piled her luggage in the trunk of her car and drove
directly up to the ranch, where she found Glenn sitting by
himself on the deck overlooking the valley. Telling him she
was going back to her own house was as difficult as she had
expected it to be. He was hurt, and as she explained why
she had to leave, he seemed to age before her eyes.

"So you see," she concluded, "much as I'd like to, there
is no way I can continue to work with Jon on your
biography. My own work is suffering too much to allow me
to go on."

"Isn't there any way you could manage to do both?" he
asked wistfully.

Linnet shook her head. "I'm afraid not. I'm way behind
on *A Summer Rhapsody*. Just meeting my deadline is going
to be a full-time job. Besides that, my editor didn't like the
work I've done on it already. Large parts of it will have to
be rewritten."

That was true. Linnet's editor had been surprised, even
shocked when she read Linnet's latest book. The characters, she said, were wooden and lifeless. It was as though
Linnet had used up all her zest for love elsewhere and had
come to the typewriter each day drained of feeling.

It was a shrewd guess, Linnet had thought at the time, for
that was exactly what had happened. Loving Jon so desperately had sapped her strength.

"Surely that doesn't mean you have to leave here,"

Glenn argued. "If you spend the afternoons working on your own book, instead of working with Jon, I'm sure you could finish it in time. At least here you wouldn't have to cook or do any housework."

If it hadn't been for Jon, Linnet would have agreed. But, if it hadn't been for Jon, she wouldn't be in this predicament, she reminded herself. As it was, she couldn't stay in the same house with him.

"That way we could still have our mornings together," Glenn added.

"I'll miss our mornings as much as you will," she told him. "But I just can't stay here any longer." Tears filled her eyes, but she forced herself to harden her heart.

"I'm an old man," Glenn said slowly, "and I know I haven't much time left. I had hoped . . ."

Linnet hated it when he talked like that. She had to fight back her tears. She didn't want Glenn to know how upset she was, or how close she was to giving in.

"It's Jon, isn't it?" he asked suddenly. He gave her a penetrating look. "He's done something to hurt you."

For a moment, Linnet thought of telling Glenn everything. In a way, it would be a relief to tell him. Then she knew that she couldn't. It would only hurt him further to know that his grandson was driving her away.

"No," she protested quickly. "It's nothing like that. I've simply got to get my book done. That's all there is to it."

"Have you told him yet?"

"No, I wanted to talk to you first."

"He'll be sorry to hear that you're leaving."

"He doesn't really need help with this book," she said. "I think he only agreed to collaborate with me to make you happy."

"I wasn't thinking of the book," Glenn said surprisingly. "I think he'll miss you as much as I will."

Linnet laughed, trying not to sound bitter. "I doubt that

he'll miss me at all." She looked at her watch. "He should be in the library. I think I'll go tell him now."

"After that I suppose you'll have to go back to Santa Barbara," Glenn said. There was a pathetic resignation in his voice.

"I'm afraid I must," she said gently.

"But you'll be back as soon as you can?" he asked with the eagerness of a child.

"As soon as I can," she promised.

"Good. I want to hear all about your trip to New York."

He tried to smile, but she could tell that he was as unhappy as she was. They both knew things could never be the same again. She gave him a quick kiss, then ran inside the house before she burst into the tears that had been threatening since she had walked out onto the deck and seen him sitting there alone.

Rather shakily, Linnet hurried upstairs to pack the rest of her clothes before she went in search of Jon. The routine of folding her things and placing them in the suitcase helped her to pull herself together. She knew she was going to need to be calm when she faced him.

When she finally felt composed, she went back downstairs. Jon was in the library. She looked in the door and saw him sitting at his desk, and she was suddenly, gloriously, angry. Jon had put her in the position of having to hurt Glenn, and she wasn't going to forgive him for that.

She was grateful for her anger. It meant she wouldn't break down in front of him and make an even bigger fool of herself than she already had.

She walked into the room, stopped in front of his desk, and waited for him to look up.

"You're back," he said in a flat voice. He put down his pencil and looked up at her intently, trying to find some encouragement in her face. He was afraid to let her see how glad he was that she had finally returned. The last time he had seen her, she had closed the door in his face. He wasn't going to risk that again.

Linnet looked back at him steadily. His face was impassive. She didn't have any idea whether he was glad to see her or not.

"Obviously," she said coolly.

"Grandfather missed you. He's talked of practically nothing but you since you left."

Did you miss me? she wanted to ask. She knew it was a question better left unsaid. The answer would only hurt her.

"And I missed him too," she said instead. Her voice softened a little as she spoke.

"You were gone long enough." His words were something of an accusation. "What could you have done in New York for six days? Three-hour lunches and late-night dinners after the theater, I suppose."

She shrugged nonchalantly. She had done none of those things, but she wasn't going to tell him that. Let him think she had lived it up.

"I had meetings and conferences, that sort of thing," she said vaguely.

"Well, now you're back and there's a lot of work to do on the book. I've got some ideas about how we can combine your approach and mine."

"I'm only back for a few minutes."

She had been tempted to listen to his ideas. Then she realized what a waste of time it would be. He had claimed to be interested in collaborating with her before, but when they got down to brass tacks, he had always let her know that her work had no place in his book. *His book!* It had always been *his* book, never *their* book, and it always would be.

He leaned back in his chair and stared up at her with narrowed eyes. "Where are you going now?"

"Home," she said simply. She was glad to see that he looked disconcerted.

"Home!" he exclaimed. "You can't go home. What about Grandfather? What about the book?"

"I've already explained to your grandfather why I'm leaving," she told him quietly. "As for the book, you don't need my help. In fact, I'm sure you'd be happier without it."

He picked up his pencil and began toying with it.

"You may have explained to Grandfather why you're leaving, but you haven't told me. And I'd like to know."

"I'm leaving because I have my own commitments and obligations to honor," she told him glibly. She had rehearsed this several times. "When I agreed to work with you, I thought I could do both. Now I see that I can't. It's as simple as that." She turned, went over to her desk, and began putting what few things were hers in her purse.

Jon stood up then. Linnet felt herself tense. She couldn't help herself. He was so big and overpowering. She forced herself to continue putting things calmly in her pocketbook.

"You're throwing away our working arrangement?" He sounded incredulous. "You're running out on the book?"

"I'm hardly running out on the book," she retorted icily, "since I never really had anything to do with it." She turned to look at him. "Let's face it, Jon. You never really wanted my help. You think my kind of writing is beneath you, and you've reminded me of that every time you got the chance."

Decisively she closed the desk drawers.

"The most we ever achieved was an uneasy truce, and even then, all I ever did was sit around and twiddle my thumbs while you tried to decide what to do with me! That's not what I call a working arrangement."

"I can understand your running out on the book," he said, leaning on the desk. "I can even understand your running out on me."

"Running out on you?" she repeated in astonishment. "What is that supposed to mean?"

"I thought there was something special between us." He stared at her, and for one sweet moment Linnet allowed herself to hope. "You enjoyed my kisses and the way I touched you, just as I enjoyed it when you touched me."

At his words, color flooded her face. "You wanted to have an affair and I didn't. Is that what you call something special?" Disappointment combined with anger to lend scorn to her voice.

He shrugged. "You can make fun of it all you want, but there is, or rather was, something special in the way we responded to each other."

How true that was, she thought a little drearily. True or not, she couldn't let him know that the way they responded to each other was one of the things that was driving her from the ranch, that and his belief that she based her love scenes on her own life. She had no intention of letting him know how much he had hurt her. Her heartache, like her love, was private.

"Perhaps," she conceded in her most worldly voice. "However, it's hardly enough to keep me here when I have other, more important things to do."

Something flickered in his eyes. "All right," he said evenly. "I can understand that. But I can't understand your running out on Grandfather. Don't you understand how important you are to him, how important you've made yourself to him? You owe it to him to stay."

"I've explained to him why I'm leaving," she said steadily. "He understands. He also knows that I'll be back to see him whenever I can."

Jon flung himself back into his chair. "All right then, go," he said curtly. He bent over his papers to hide his sudden feeling of desolation.

Linnet stared down at his bent head in dismayed surprise.

She had wanted to get in the last word, but he had denied her even that. She hesitated for a moment, trying to think of a good exit line. Then she gave up the attempt. What was the point? This was the end of whatever she and Jon had shared.

She turned and hurried out the door. Her anger had evaporated as suddenly as it had come. Now all she felt was an overpowering sadness for the old man sitting alone on the deck, sadness for the love that had never been allowed to flower.

The tears she had refused to let fall earlier now slipped down her face. Almost blindly, she got into her car and shut the door behind her. She brushed away her tears, then drove unsteadily away from the ranch.

Halfway down the mountain, misery overcame her. Her tears were falling so fast that she couldn't see. She pulled over, leaned on the steering wheel, and sobbed. She felt as though her world had ended.

Inside the ranch house, in the library, Jon suddenly threw his pencil across the room and swore aloud. He pushed the chair away from the desk and got to his feet. Angrily he stalked down the hall, across the living room, and out onto the deck. Glenn was still sitting there by himself.

"She's gone," Jon said flatly.

He dropped into a chair across from his grandfather. Ever since Linnet had left six days before, the house had seemed empty, as though something vital, some part of him, had gone with her.

"You mean you let her go?" Glenn sounded more shocked than surprised.

"Of course I let her go," Jon snapped. "What else could I do?"

"You could have told her you love her," Glenn said simply. "You do love her, don't you?"

Jon stared at him angrily. "Yes, I love her."

The words came out reluctantly, as though Jon wasn't sure he wanted to say them.

"But I don't see . . ."

"Go after her then," Glenn urged. "Go after her or you'll regret it for the rest of your life."

The urgency of Glenn's voice seemed to get through to Jon. He got up and paced restlessly across the deck.

"I can't do that," he objected. "She doesn't care anything at all for me. She as much as told me so. Her work means more to her than I do."

Glenn looked at him with amused exasperation. "Of course she loves you. It's written all over her."

Jon looked at his grandfather and shook his head doubtfully. "I don't know."

"Well, I do know. I've been sitting out here for the past hour working it out. Why do you think she's leaving?"

"Because of her damn books," Jon said grimly.

Glenn raised his eyes to the heavens. "She's leaving because she can't bear to be in the same house with you any longer. It's tearing her apart."

Jon stopped pacing. Hope was beginning to show in his face.

"Do you think so?"

"I know so," Glenn said firmly. "She's in love with you. Only a fool could miss it and you, my boy, have been a fool."

Jon began fitting the pieces together, pieces that had always perplexed him before.

"You may be right," he said slowly.

"Of course I'm right. Now go after her. Hurry!"

Jon smiled then, and in that smile his grandfather could see all the brightness of the sun. Without another word, Jon rushed through the house. From his spot on the deck, Glenn could hear the car door slam shut and the engine of Jon's sports car spring to life. He leaned back in his chair with a feeling of satisfaction. He was exhausted, but he had done his best for Jon and Linnet.

Young people, he thought with amused tolerance. Whoever had said that youth was wasted on the young was right.

Now all he could do was wait, wait and hope that it wasn't too late for them to set things straight.

Jon's car raced down the mountain, careening wildly around the curves. He was going so fast that he almost passed Linnet's parked car before he saw it. He skidded to a stop, jumped out, and yanked open her car door. What he saw tore at his heart. Linnet was slumped over the steering wheel, crying as though her heart had broken. She raised a tear-stained face as he said her name.

"What do you want?" she asked angrily. She didn't like being caught with all her defenses down. "What do you want?" she repeated angrily.

"You," he answered simply. "I can't let you go." He gently pushed her across the seat and slid behind the wheel.

"You don't really have much choice," she told him with a show of spirit. She reached into the glove compartment, took out a tissue, and wiped away her tears. "Now, if you don't mind, I'd like you to get out of my car. I'm going home."

"You're not going home until you hear what I have to say. Then if you still want to go home, you can. But I warn you, I'll follow you. And I'll keep following you until . . ."

"Please, Jon," she interrupted with desperation. "I don't want to listen to whatever you have to say. I want to go home."

She had to get away from him. If she didn't, she was either going to burst into tears again or reach over and put her arms around him. Neither seemed like a good idea.

"You can't go home. Not yet, anyway," he pointed out smugly. "I'm in the driver's seat. Please Linnet, just listen for a moment while . . .

"All right. If you won't get out of this car, I will."

She grasped the door handle and would have opened it if he hadn't reached across her and captured her hand.

"What are you going to do, walk back to Santa Barbara?"

"If I have to, yes." She pulled her hand from his with a jerk.

"You're being ridiculous," he told her. "You're not going anywhere until you hear what I have to say."

"Oh yes, I am!"

This time she managed to get the door open. She would have gotten out of the car if he hadn't taken hold of her arm. She tried to shake his hand off, but he refused to let go.

"Will you please listen to me? I'm trying to tell you that I love you."

Linnet stopped trying to pry his hand loose with her fingers.

"I beg your pardon?" she said in her most polite voice.

"I said I love you. Now will you listen to what I have to say?"

She didn't answer. She just sat there, staring at him. She couldn't answer.

He moved across the seat a little closer to her and took her hand in his.

"I think I've loved you all along—ever since that moment when I saw you standing in the lobby of the Chez Nous with a birthday present in your hands," he said softly. "I just didn't realize it until you left for New York."

He touched her cheek gently with his finger. Linnet stared down at her lap. Jon slid his hand down her face until he could cup her chin, tilt her head back, and look into her eyes.

"Once you were gone, the house seemed empty; I felt empty. It was as though something of great importance had suddenly gone out of my life, and that something was you."

Linnet stared into his eyes, barely breathing. She was beginning to believe him.

"Every time I come near you," he said, sliding his large hand down to encircle her neck, "I have to stop myself from taking you in my arms. That's what I want to do now."

Slowly, he traced the outline of her lips.

"You have such a kissable mouth," he murmured. "I told you that the very first night we met. It's almost irresistibly soft and inviting."

He leaned over and touched her lips with his very lightly, very gently.

"When I think of all the time we've wasted talking and arguing when we could have been doing this . . ."

He kissed her again.

"And this."

His third kiss, though still gentle, was not as light.

"And this."

This kiss was a lingering one, and Linnet gave herself up to it with a sigh. When they finally moved apart, she drew an unsteady breath and gazed up at him happily. This was a moment she had thought would never be hers. Then her eyes clouded over.

"This isn't all there is to love," she said quietly. "I think, perhaps, you've gotten love and passion confused."

He smiled tenderly. "I don't think so. Though I admit I'm no expert when it comes to love, I can recognize passion. What I feel for you is more than passion. I love you, Linnet. I want you to marry me."

Linnet allowed herself to savor the moment. She had never experienced such complete happiness and she was sure she never would again. Jon's words had banished her heartache and replaced it with joy. She gave him a radiant smile that told him that he was loved in return.

"Please say you'll marry me," he urged her. "Say you love me. I can see it in your eyes, but I want to hear it."

"I do love you, Jon," she said. "I love you more than I ever imagined possible."

She spoke with a quiet seriousness that told him at once that something was wrong.

Her smile faded and tears filled her eyes. "But I can't marry you."

The finality in her voice was chilling.

"Why not?" he demanded.

It was an effort, but Linnet pulled away from him.

"I can't marry you," she repeated a little tiredly. "Let's just leave it at that. I really don't feel like talking about it."

"Why not?" he asked again. His voice was rougher this time. "First you say you love me, then, a moment later, you say you won't marry me. I want to know why. I have a right to know why."

She sighed. She wasn't sure she could make him understand her reasons for not marrying him. But she supposed she'd have to try. She owed him that.

"A good marriage isn't just based on physical love," she said softly. "Respect and caring have to go hand in hand if a marriage is going to last. I want my marriage to last. I have no desire to be a part of the yearly divorce statistics."

He looked at her a little blankly. "I feel the same way. I would never have asked you to marry me if I thought our marriage wouldn't last."

"You don't respect me," she pointed out quietly. "Without that respect, our marriage would never work."

"Of course I respect you." He sounded impatient.

"No, Jon," she said firmly. "You don't. You've never missed an opportunity to belittle my work, and my work is an important part of me. If you can't respect it, then you can't respect me either.''

Jon stared out the window in silence while Linnet gazed down at her hands.

Once more Jon put his arms around her and pulled her close. Linnet didn't resist but she didn't relax against him either.

"This isn't going to be easy for me," he told her somberly, "but I've got to make you understand." He cradled her in his arms and rested his cheek against her head.

"It's no use," she said as she tried to keep her body from fitting against his. She had always felt at home in his arms, but never more so than now, when she was sending him away. "You're only making this harder for both of us.''

He ignored her.

"When I first met you," he said slowly, "I admit that I had certain prejudices. I've always thought of romance novels as a waste of time. It seemed to me that any self-respecting writer ought to write about serious subjects.''

He began to stroke her hair absentmindedly. Linnet felt his hands move up and down, and his touch almost distracted her from what he was saying.

"As I got to know you," he went on a little ruefully, "I began to see that I was being unfair. You showed me that a writer's first job is to reach the reader. You do a far better job of that than I could ever do.''

Linnet stirred in his arms. If he was telling the truth, there might be a chance for them. Hope was growing within her.

"Let me finish," he commanded. "You've taught me that there's far more to life than hard facts and abstract ideas.''

Linnet looked up at him with doubtful eyes. She wanted, desperately wanted, to believe him, but she was afraid to.

"Working with you, living with you, and loving you have shown me how important love can be. I didn't realize all this at once, of course," he added as he noticed the doubt in her eyes. "But after you had gone, I had time to think, and I began to understand the importance of the things you believe in."

He leaned over and kissed her with a tenderness that brought fresh tears to her eyes.

"I also began to understand just how vital you are to my happiness. I've never been in love before," he told her earnestly. "I suppose that's why I was so slow to recognize it. But now that I know what it is, I'm not going to let you walk out of my life."

Gently, Linnet touched his face. Jon moved her hand to his lips and kissed her palm.

"When you closed the door in my face just before you left for New York," he went on in a voice that had grown dark with remembered pain, "I didn't think I could stand it."

"I was hurt," Linnet said quickly. She wanted to banish the despair from his face. "You had said some very cruel things."

He dropped her hand and his arms tightened around her again. "I know I did, and I'm sorry. I was jealous. It's that simple. I can't bear the thought of any other man touching you."

He kissed her again, possessively this time.

"It was the love scenes in your book," he confessed. "They drove me mad with jealousy. They're so realistic, so powerful. I couldn't understand how you could have written them unless . . ."

She reached up and covered his mouth with her fingers.

"No man has ever come as close to me, physically or

emotionally, as you have, Jon," she told him. "I've been waiting for a man I could love and respect, a man like you."

There was a new light in his eyes.

"Will you marry me, Linnet?" he asked humbly. "I'm hardly perfect and I'm not always easy to live with, but I promise to love you and cherish you. Please marry me."

There was anxiety in his eyes, anxiety that only she could dispel. She smiled at him.

"Yes, I'll marry you," she told him joyfully.

As she said the words, she knew she was making the right decision. She belonged with Jon; they belonged together.

"What about Grandfather's biography? Will you help me with that?"

"If you want me to," she answered.

"I want your help. In fact, I need it." He chuckled. "I just hope I can keep my mind on our work. I'd much rather be kissing you."

"In that case," she said teasingly, "perhaps we should collaborate on a romance."

He laughed. "I almost believe I could," he said. "That's how much you've taught me." His voice grew serious. "I hope you won't stop writing once we're married."

Once we're married, Linnet thought rapturously. The words sounded wonderful.

"No, I won't stop writing," she said. "In fact, I think I'll be able to write even better love stories now that I know what it's like to love and be loved in return."

She raised her eyes to his. They were glowing with happiness.

"You know, I've always wanted the same kind of happy ending that my heroines have," she confessed shyly. "I think I've found it."

He shook his head. "This isn't the end of our love story, it's the beginning."

He lowered his lips, and his kiss conveyed a promise of things to come. When Linnet finally pulled away, she was breathless.

Jon looked deep into her eyes.

"I love you," he said. "I'll love you forever."

Cradling her close, he turned the car around, and they started back to the ranch where they would make a frail old man very happy.

Silhouette Romance

IT'S YOUR OWN SPECIAL TIME
*Contemporary romances for today's women.
Each month, six very special love stories will be yours
from SILHOUETTE.*

$1.75 each

☐ 100 Stanford	☐ 128 Hampson	☐ 157 Vitek	☐ 185 Hampson
☐ 101 Hardy	☐ 129 Converse	☐ 158 Reynolds	☐ 186 Howard
☐ 102 Hastings	☐ 130 Hardy	☐ 159 Tracy	☐ 187 Scott
☐ 103 Cork	☐ 131 Stanford	☐ 160 Hampson	☐ 188 Cork
☐ 104 Vitek	☐ 132 Wisdom	☐ 161 Trent	☐ 189 Stephens
☐ 105 Eden	☐ 133 Rowe	☐ 162 Ashby	☐ 190 Hampson
☐ 106 Dailey	☐ 134 Charles	☐ 163 Roberts	☐ 191 Browning
☐ 107 Bright	☐ 135 Logan	☐ 164 Browning	☐ 192 John
☐ 108 Hampson	☐ 136 Hampson	☐ 165 Young	☐ 193 Trent
☐ 109 Vernon	☐ 137 Hunter	☐ 166 Wisdom	☐ 194 Barry
☐ 110 Trent	☐ 138 Wilson	☐ 167 Hunter	☐ 195 Dailey
☐ 111 South	☐ 139 Vitek	☐ 168 Carr	☐ 196 Hampson
☐ 112 Stanford	☐ 140 Erskine	☐ 169 Scott	☐ 197 Summers
☐ 113 Browning	☐ 142 Browning	☐ 170 Ripy	☐ 198 Hunter
☐ 114 Michaels	☐ 143 Roberts	☐ 171 Hill	☐ 199 Roberts
☐ 115 John	☐ 144 Goforth	☐ 172 Browning	☐ 200 Lloyd
☐ 116 Lindley	☐ 145 Hope	☐ 173 Camp	☐ 201 Starr
☐ 117 Scott	☐ 146 Michaels	☐ 174 Sinclair	☐ 202 Hampson
☐ 118 Dailey	☐ 147 Hampson	☐ 175 Jarrett	☐ 203 Browning
☐ 119 Hampson	☐ 148 Cork	☐ 176 Vitek	☐ 204 Carroll
☐ 120 Carroll	☐ 149 Saunders	☐ 177 Dailey	☐ 205 Maxam
☐ 121 Langan	☐ 150 Major	☐ 178 Hampson	☐ 206 Manning
☐ 122 Scofield	☐ 151 Hampson	☐ 179 Beckman	☐ 207 Windham
☐ 123 Sinclair	☐ 152 Halston	☐ 180 Roberts	☐ 208 Halston
☐ 124 Beckman	☐ 153 Dailey	☐ 181 Terrill	☐ 209 LaDame
☐ 125 Bright	☐ 154 Beckman	☐ 182 Clay	☐ 210 Eden
☐ 126 St. George	☐ 155 Hampson	☐ 183 Stanley	☐ 211 Walters
☐ 127 Roberts	☐ 156 Sawyer	☐ 184 Hardy	☐ 212 Young

$1.95 each

☐ 213 Dailey	☐ 217 Vitek	☐ 221 Browning	☐ 225 St. George
☐ 214 Hampson	☐ 218 Hunter	☐ 222 Carroll	☐ 226 Hampson
☐ 215 Roberts	☐ 219 Cork	☐ 223 Summers	☐ 227 Beckman
☐ 216 Saunders	☐ 220 Hampson	☐ 224 Langan	☐ 228 King

Silhouette Romance

$1.95 each

☐ 229 Thornton	☐ 254 Palmer	☐ 279 Ashby	☐ 304 Cork
☐ 230 Stevens	☐ 255 Smith	☐ 280 Roberts	☐ 305 Browning
☐ 231 Dailey	☐ 256 Hampson	☐ 281 Lovan	☐ 306 Gordon
☐ 232 Hampson	☐ 257 Hunter	☐ 282 Halldorson	☐ 307 Wildman
☐ 233 Vernon	☐ 258 Ashby	☐ 283 Payne	☐ 308 Young
☐ 234 Smith	☐ 259 English	☐ 284 Young	☐ 309 Hardy
☐ 235 James	☐ 260 Martin	☐ 285 Gray	☐ 310 Hunter
☐ 236 Maxam	☐ 261 Saunders	☐ 286 Cork	☐ 311 Gray
☐ 237 Wilson	☐ 262 John	☐ 287 Joyce	☐ 312 Vernon
☐ 238 Cork	☐ 263 Wilson	☐ 288 Smith	☐ 313 Rainville
☐ 239 McKay	☐ 264 Vine	☐ 289 Saunders	☐ 314 Palmer
☐ 240 Hunter	☐ 265 Adams	☐ 290 Hunter	☐ 315 Smith
☐ 241 Wisdom	☐ 266 Trent	☐ 291 McKay	☐ 316 Macomber
☐ 242 Brooke	☐ 267 Chase	☐ 292 Browning	☐ 317 Langan
☐ 243 Saunders	☐ 268 Hunter	☐ 293 Morgan	☐ 318 Herrington
☐ 244 Sinclair	☐ 269 Smith	☐ 294 Cockcroft	☐ 319 Lloyd
☐ 245 Trent	☐ 270 Camp	☐ 295 Vernon	☐ 320 Brooke
☐ 246 Carroll	☐ 271 Allison	☐ 296 Paige	☐ 321 Glenn
☐ 247 Halldorson	☐ 272 Forrest	☐ 297 Young	☐ 322 Hunter
☐ 248 St. George	☐ 273 Beckman	☐ 298 Hunter	☐ 323 Browning
☐ 249 Scofield	☐ 274 Roberts	☐ 299 Roberts	☐ 324 Maxam
☐ 250 Hampson	☐ 275 Browning	☐ 300 Stephens	☐ 325 Smith
☐ 251 Wilson	☐ 276 Vernon	☐ 301 Palmer	☐ 326 Lovan
☐ 252 Roberts	☐ 277 Wilson	☐ 302 Smith	☐ 327 James
☐ 253 James	☐ 278 Hunter	☐ 303 Langan	

Silhouette Romance

Coming Next Month

PASSION FLOWER
by Diana Palmer

•

CIRCUMSTANTIAL EVIDENCE
by Annette Broadrick

•

CRYSTAL ANGEL
by Olivia Ferrell

•

MAGGIE'S MISCELLANY
by Kasey Michaels

•

THE GOLDEN ROSE
by Betsy McCarty

•

A TANGLE OF RAINBOWS
by Laurie Paige